SHERLOCK HOLMES'S BAKER STREET BOYS

Anthony Read studied at the Central School of Speech and Drama in London, and was an actor-manager at the age of eighteen. He worked in advertising, journalism and publishing and as a television producer before becoming a full-time writer. Anthony has more than two hundred screen credits to his name, for programmes that include *Sherlock Holmes*, *The Professionals* and *Doctor Who*. He has also written non-fiction, and won the Wingate Literary Prize for *Kristallnacht*.

The Baker Street Boys books, *The Case of the Disappearing Detective*, *The Case of the Captive Clairvoyant*, *The Case of the Ranjipur Ruby* and *The Case of the Limehouse Laundry*, are based on Anthony's original television series for children, broadcast by the BBC in the 1980s, for which he won the Writers' Guild TV Award. The series was inspired by references to the "Baker Street Irregulars", a group of young crime-solvers who helped the detective Sherlock Holmes in the classic stories by Sir Arthur Conan Doyle.

THE CASE OF THE
LIMEHOUSE
LAUNDRY

ANTHONY READ

Illustrated by
DAVID FRANKLAND

WALKER
BOOKS

First published 2007 by Walker Books Ltd
87 Vauxhall Walk, London SE11 5HJ

2 4 6 8 10 9 7 5 3 1

This book has been typeset in Garamond Book

Printed and bound in Great Britain by J.H. Haynes & Co. Ltd

British Library Cataloguing in Publication Data:
a catalogue record for this book is available from the British Library

ISBN 978-1-4063-0341-4

www.walkerbooks.co.uk

Contents

"Violets! Lovely violets! Buy a posy for your lady, sir?"

The little flower girl picked up a neatly tied bunch of blooms from the tray around her neck. She smiled appealingly.

"Only tuppence, sir. Only tuppence a bunch... Thank you, kind sir."

Across the street a sinister figure watched from inside a black carriage and raised one gloved hand in a signal.

The girl walked on. She hardly noticed the van as it drew up alongside her. There was nothing unusual about a delivery van – the streets of London were full of delivery vans. She had to stop and wait as the driver and his mate hopped down and swung open the rear doors, blocking the pavement for a moment.

There was a sudden flurry of activity, hidden by the open doors before they were closed again and the van drove off. Across the street, the black carriage moved quietly away in the opposite direction. Where the van had stood, a few posies and nosegays lay scattered in the gutter. But there was no sign of the girl.

She had disappeared.

LOOKING FOR LILY

The morning mist floated in the air like smoke from a bonfire as Rosie trudged through the streets of London carrying her empty flower tray. She had left HQ early as usual, while the rest of the Baker Street Boys were still sleeping – except for Queenie, that is. Queenie, as usual, had left her bed to make sure Rosie had a drink of water and a piece of bread to nibble before she set out on her daily walk to Covent Garden market.

"It's a long way, there and back," Queenie always told her. "If you don't have somethin' to keep your strength up, you'll be tired out afore the day's really started."

The streets near HQ were all quiet as Rosie left. In the houses, curtains were drawn and shutters closed as people slept. The only traffic was a few early shopkeepers, already on their way back from market with the day's fresh fish or meat or vegetables. Rosie passed the old lamp-lighter reaching up with his long pole to turn off the gas in the street lamps, and the postman making his first delivery of the day. PC Higgins, looking enormous in his tall helmet and heavy cape, gave her a wave and a cheery greeting – he was happy to be heading back to the police station after a long night alone on his beat. But there was no sign yet of the crowds of people who would throng the pavements later in the day, nor of the carriages and cabs and carts that would pack the roadways.

There was no sign either of Rosie's friend Lily, another flower girl, who was about the same age as herself and almost as pretty. In fact they looked so alike that people sometimes confused them with each other, though Lily's fair hair was straight and she wore it tied back in a pony-tail, while Rosie's tumbled down to her shoulders in golden curls. The two girls liked to walk to and from the market together each morning, chatting and joking, and Lily was usually waiting for Rosie on the corner near the Baker Street Bazaar. Today, however, she was nowhere to be seen. Rosie waited for a few minutes, looking up and down the street, but then shrugged and set off on her own. She did not want to be late, or the best flowers would have gone.

As Rosie got closer to Covent Garden, the streets became busier. All through the night, hundreds of carts and vans and wagons had trundled in from the countryside, piled high with fruit and vegetables. Each cart brought a fresh splash of colour to the scene – green cabbages, lettuces, peas and beans, milky-white turnips, parsnips and cauliflowers, bright orange carrots, shiny red apples and cherries. Only the potatoes, still caked with dirt, were dull and brown in their coarse muddy sacks. There were no flowers to be seen, though. They came to the market separately, in closed vans. Many of them had arrived in London by train from faraway parts of England, packed in boxes or baskets to protect them from harm.

Porters had been working hard all night, unloading the produce and carrying it into the great market halls, where traders sold it to greengrocers and hotels and restaurants. Now the empty carts were leaving, heading back to their farms before the city woke up. The big horses were eager to get home, and they moved faster with no heavy loads to pull. Rosie had to dodge between the carts, sometimes flattening herself against a building or ducking into a doorway to avoid being squashed or run over by the big wooden wheels with their iron rims grinding on the cobblestones.

In the Piazza, the big square in front of the market halls, there was less danger from the heavy wagons. But Rosie still had to keep her wits about her as she threaded her way between the hundreds of smaller carts and vans and barrows, coming and going in all directions, pulled and pushed by horses, donkeys and men. Somewhere a donkey started braying, a loud, hoarse *hee-haw* that was answered by all the other donkeys, drowning out every other sound in the noisy square.

"Oi! Mind yer bloomin' back! Outta the way!"

The shout came from a lean young man who

was trotting past, balancing a tower of nine or ten circular baskets on his head. Because of the din the donkeys were making, Rosie had not heard him coming.

"Wotcha, Charlie!" Rosie called. "Sorry, mate!"

Charlie gave her a cheerful wave but did not slow down or stop. The tower of baskets swayed gracefully as he swerved round her, but it stayed upright. Such a balancing act would have earnt a round of applause on the stage of Mr Trump's Imperial Music Hall. But here in Covent Garden no one took any notice – it was just how all the porters carried baskets and boxes. All over the market, men and boys were doing the same thing, trotting busily along without using their hands to hold or even to steady their loads. For all their bustle and haste, they never seemed to drop anything.

Rosie hurried across the Piazza to the Floral Hall, where flowers were bought and sold. Many other girls and women were heading there too, and Rosie kept hoping to see Lily among them. But there was no sign of her friend as she entered the hall, with its high glass roof and walls, and elegant green ironwork shaped like a huge lady's fan. Inside, the smell was overpowering as the scent from thousands and thousands of blooms mingled together. There were flowers and plants everywhere, stacked high on stalls waiting to be sold, or moving along the aisles on trolleys and barrows as florists wheeled them away to stock their shops.

"Wotcha, me little Rosie! 'Ow's it goin', then?" an older girl greeted her with a grin. This was Eliza, who must have been sixteen or even seventeen and wore a battered black straw hat perched on top of her head like a lost bird, and a tartan shawl around her shoulders. Eliza had been selling flowers for years, from the steps of St Paul's Church on the Piazza, where she could shelter under the porch when it was raining and didn't have far to walk. She lived in an alley off the market with her father, a dustman who beat her when he was drunk – which was most of the time. But she was always cheerful, and all the other girls looked up to her as their leader.

"On your own today?" Eliza asked. "Where's Lily, then?"

"Dunno," Rosie replied. "Thought she might be here already."

"No. Ain't seen hide nor hair of her. And I would have, if she was here. Eliza don't miss much in this 'ere market."

"P'raps she's took sick," Rosie said.

"Yeh, p'raps there's somethin' goin' round. There's two or three other girls ain't turned up this last day or two wivout a word."

"Is that right?" Rosie was sorry to think of Lily being ill. "I'll look in at her place on my way home," she said, "to see if she's all right."

"Good girl," said Eliza, heading for the door. "She's lucky to have a chum like you. You take care of yourself now."

Rosie moved through the market stalls, choosing small flowers which she would make into nosegays and posies for ladies, and button-holes for gentlemen. All the time she kept an eye open for Lily, hoping to see her come hurrying into the hall. But Lily did not appear, and when Rosie had filled her tray and spent all the money she had saved for her stock, she set off to walk back home on her own.

*   *   *

Back at HQ, the secret cellar where they all lived, the rest of the Boys were finishing breakfast when Rosie stumbled down the steps with tears streaming down her face. They all looked at her in alarm, and Queenie and Beaver quickly got up and hurried over.

"Why, Rosie, love! What's up?" Queenie said, putting an arm round her.

"Has somebody hurt you?" Beaver asked, looking concerned.

"It's Lily," Rosie sobbed. "Somethin' terrible's happened to her. I know it has."

"What?" asked Beaver.

"I dunno. That's the trouble. I dunno." And she wept even harder as Queenie hugged her and tried to comfort her.

Wiggins roused himself from his special chair and went to her.

"Now then, now then!" he said. "Can't have this. You better tell me all about it, and we'll see what's to be done. Right?"

Rosie nodded, sniffed and wiped her eyes and nose on her sleeve.

"It's Lily," she began.

"Yeah, you said that already. What about her?"

"Well, we always look out for each other. And we always walks to Covent Garden together of a mornin' to buy our stock. Always."

"Yes?"

"Well, this mornin' she didn't come."

"P'raps she fancied a day off," Sparrow said.

"Couldn't be bothered to wake up," Shiner chipped in. "I know 'ow she feels."

"P'raps she's took sick," Gertie suggested. "She never looks strong to me."

"That's what Eliza at the market said," Rosie replied. "So I called round at her place on my way home. She wasn't there. Her ma said she never come home last night."

"Oh, lawks," said Queenie. "That don't sound good."

"Hang on," said Wiggins. "We don't know nothing yet. She might have run away."

"That's right," agreed Beaver. "She might have. I did. That's how I come to be here. And if she's run off, she wouldn't have gone home last night, would she? 'Cos she wouldn't want to, so she'd have gone somewhere else, and if she'd gone somewhere else…"

"Beaver!" Wiggins stopped him before he got completely carried away.

"Oh, sorry. I just thought…"

"No, no," sobbed Rosie. "She wouldn't have run away. Not without telling me. I'm her friend. She tells me everything."

"I bet somebody's bashed her over the head and took her flower money," Shiner said with a mischievous glint in his eye.

Rosie burst into fresh tears at the thought of her friend lying hurt and alone.

"Shiner!" Queenie snapped. "That's enough. Rosie's upset enough without you makin' it worse."

Shiner shrugged and snatched the last piece of bread from the table before grabbing his box of shoe brushes and boot polish and heading out of the door to start work.

"Just keep your eyes open for any sign of Lily!" Queenie shouted after him.

"And that goes for everybody, right?" said Wiggins. "We'll all look out for her."

"There," Queenie told Rosie, "dry your eyes now and get on with makin' your posies and buttonholes. If you don't sell 'em, you won't have no money to buy no more tomorrow, will you?"

Rosie shook her head, sat down at the table and picked up the fine wire she used to tie the flowers together in her own special way. In a moment, her nimble fingers were fashioning them into little bunches, the prettiest to be found anywhere on the streets of London. Being busy helped her to stop thinking quite so much about what might have happened to Lily – as Queenie had known it would. But she didn't forget her, and when Rosie walked along the street with her tray round her neck later that morning, she kept looking in all directions, hoping to see some sign of her chum.

As Rosie was so worried about Lily, Wiggins sent the other Boys off to look around and to ask if anyone had seen her. He and Beaver went to find Lily's mother, to see if they could find out any more from her.

"That's what Mr Holmes would do," Wiggins said. "He'd ask lots and lots of questions, and then he'd know what was going on."

"What *is* goin' on?" asked Beaver.

"I don't know, do I?" Wiggins sighed heavily. "That's why I gotta ask the questions."

"Oh. Right. What questions?"

"Never mind." Wiggins sighed again. "Just leave the talking to me. And while I'm talking, I want you to keep your eyes peeled and see if you can spot any clues."

Beaver nodded eagerly, pleased to be given something useful to do. Then his face clouded again.

"What sort of clues?" he asked.

"How should I know? Anything what don't look right. Right?"

"Right."

"OK, then. Here we go."

They had arrived at the house where Rosie had told them Lily lived in one room with her mother and brothers and sisters. It was a rickety old building that looked ready to be pulled down – if it didn't fall down first. A woman was leaning against the open front door, holding a small child on her hip. From inside the house came the sounds of other children crying and fighting.

"Are you Lily's ma?" asked Wiggins.

The woman stared at him suspiciously, through dull eyes that seemed too big for her thin, tired face.

"Who wants to know?" she replied.

"We do. I'm Wiggins, he's Beaver. We're pals of Rosie – you know Rosie, Lily's friend?"

"Yeah, I know Rosie. She's a good girl, she is. She wouldn't run off and leave her poor old ma like my Lily has, selfish little cow."

"How d'you know she's run off, Mrs er…?"

"Pool. Mrs Pool. Well, she never come 'ome last night, did she? And I ain't heard a word from her since."

She coughed, a hollow, racking cough that shook her bony shoulders inside her threadbare grey dress and creased her face with pain. She dabbed at her mouth with the end of the sack that was tied around her waist to serve as an apron. The noise of children fighting turned into screams. Mrs Pool turned and walked wearily into the house. Wiggins and Beaver followed her.

"Stop it! Stop it, all of you!" she cried.

The noise did not stop.

"Stop it!" she repeated. "Please!" Her face crumpled and she began to cry.

There was a confused heap of children piled on the floor of the bare room. Legs, arms, elbows, heads were sticking out of it, bobbing and flailing, wrestling and punching, kicking and biting. It was impossible to tell just how many children there were, but none of them paid any attention to their mother's cries – even if they could hear them over their own yells and screams. Wiggins and Beaver looked at Mrs Pool, standing weeping and helpless. Wiggins took a deep breath and shouted as loudly as he knew how.

"QUIET!!"

Wiggins's voice filled the room, echoing off the walls and stunning the fighting children into silence. He and Beaver bent over them, disentangling limbs, separating them from each other and hauling them to their feet. When they had done, they found that there were four children, two boys and two girls, who stared at them with open mouths, shocked at the sudden appearance of the big boys.

"That's more like it," said Beaver. "Couldn't hear meself think with all that racket."

"Right," said Wiggins. "Now stand over there and don't say nothing till I says you can."

Beaver lined them up along the wall and inspected them. They looked as though they were aged between six and about nine or ten, though they were all small and skinny, with hollow cheeks in pale faces. Their clothes were ragged and none of them had any shoes or stockings on their feet. But although they were dusty from rolling on the floor, they were generally clean and their eyes were bright.

"Blimey, missus," said Wiggins, turning to Mrs Pool. "Are they always like that?"

The mother nodded sadly. "Truth is," she said, "I can't control 'em, not since my old man left me on my own. 'Specially wiv me bein' not so well." And she coughed again, holding her chest to stop the pain.

"P'raps that's why Lily done a bunk," said Beaver. "I mean, if this lot are always fightin' and screamin', p'raps she couldn't stand it no more. And if she couldn't stand it no more, she might have thought, you know… I mean, if she thought, well … and then she might have thought…"

"No," Mrs Pool interrupted him. "Lily's always been real good wiv the little 'uns. Ain't that right, kids?"

"Yeah," the older girl said. "We loves our Lily. And she loves us."

Mrs Pool started crying again. "I dunno what I'm gonna do wivout her," she sobbed. "Or her flower money. Oh, if only I hadn't spoke so sharp to her yesterday mornin'…"

The four children rushed over, hugging her tight and tugging at her skirt.

"Don't cry, Ma," the older girl said. "It weren't your fault."

"Yes, it was. It was – I should never have told her off like that."

"Shouted at her, did you?" asked Wiggins. "What was it about?"

"Nothin', really. I told her to get a move on or she'd miss the best flowers."

"But she was upset?"

"No more than usual."

"Did she threaten to run away?"

"She was always threatenin' to run away. Every time we had cross words. Didn't mean nothin'."

"Did she say where she might go?"

"Only the usual. Said if I wasn't careful she'd go and live with some gang she knew about. Where there weren't no grown-ups to boss her about."

Wiggins and Beaver exchanged glances.

"Did she say what this gang was called?"

"Oh, I can't remember. Something to do with Baker Street, I think."

"The Baker Street Boys?"

"That's it! The Baker Street Boys. Though why my little girl should want to go with a gang of boys beats me."

"Well, as it 'appens," Wiggins told her, "three of the Boys are girls, if you know what I mean."

"No, I don't." Mrs Pool looked puzzled. "How d'you know?"

"'Cos we're the Baker Street Boys," said Beaver proudly. "Or at least, we're two of 'em. See, there's another five of us and…"

"And you don't have to fret no more about Lily," Wiggins said. "Not now you've got the Baker Street Boys on the case. We'll soon find her for you."

CHINESE ACROBATICS

All through the day the Baker Street Boys searched for any sign of the missing flower girl. They asked everyone they knew – Bert, the stage doorkeeper at the theatre; Sarge at the Bazaar; old Ant the baked potato man; all the youngsters who did odd jobs on the streets, holding horses' heads, sweeping crossings, running messages – but they found nothing and no one knew anything. One or two people thought they might have seen Lily selling flowers during the morning, but they couldn't be sure.

By late afternoon Sparrow had to stop searching and go to work at the Imperial Music Hall. Wearing his call boy's short jacket with its rows of shiny buttons, he had to look after the performers during the evening show, running errands, carrying messages, fetching drinks and snacks from the bar, whatever the artistes needed.

There was one group of artistes, however, who didn't seem to need him to fetch food. When a strange aroma wafted through the backstage area, Sparrow followed his nose to track it down. He had never smelled anything quite like it before and he had no idea where it was coming from until he saw smoke seeping underneath the door of the biggest dressing room. Something was burning.

"Fire! Fire!" he yelled.

Grabbing the nearest fire bucket from the corridor, he opened the door, ready to throw the water on the fire. The smoke in the room made his eyes sting, but through it he could see the troupe of Chinese acrobats who were on the bill that week. There were four men and a boy of about Sparrow's own age. All were dressed in brightly coloured silk clothes, mainly blue and yellow and red, and all wore their shiny black hair in long pigtails hanging down their backs. They were sitting cross-legged on the floor around a little paraffin stove, on which they were frying something in a pan of hot fat that was sizzling and smoking. They looked up in surprise when Sparrow opened the door, then shouted in alarm when they saw the bucket he was holding.

"No, no! Stop!" the Chinese boy cried. "No fire. Only cook."

Sparrow put the bucket down and stared at the stove and the collection of pots and dishes on the floor. What they contained was not like any food he had ever seen, and he wondered if it tasted as strange as it smelled.

"Food," the Chinese boy said. "Taste good. You want try?"

Sparrow could never turn down the chance of food, so he nodded, if a little nervously, as the boy beckoned him towards the dishes. He looked for a spoon or a fork but could not see either.

"How, er, how d'you eat it?" he asked.

The Chinese boy grinned and pointed to some little sticks made from ivory.

"Chopsticks," he said. "See. Li help." He pointed one finger at his chest. "Me Li."

Sparrow nodded and patted his own chest. "Me Sparrow," he said.

"Spa-ow," the lad repeated, struggling to say the "r" sound. "Good."

Li took two of the little sticks in one hand, deftly picked up a piece of food with them and held it out. Sparrow thought this was very clever, but as he was trying to work out how it was done, the boy nodded to him to open his mouth, then quickly popped in the morsel of meat. Sparrow bit into it cautiously. At first it tasted good, full of strange flavours that made his tongue tingle, but when he swallowed, it suddenly seemed to explode. His mouth and lips were burning. His face turned bright red and his eyes started to stream.

"You like?" Li asked with a grin. "Plenty spice, yes?"

Sparrow couldn't answer. He looked around the room frantically, then spotted the bucket of water and plunged his face into it. When he surfaced, the Chinese acrobats were laughing hard. Then Sparrow heard a familiar voice booming out from the doorway behind him.

"I apprehended your alarum." It was the plummy voice of the theatre manager, Mr Trump.

"Where is the location of the conflagration?"

"Eh?"

"The fire, you nincompoop. Where is the fire?"

Sparrow was still gasping for breath, but he managed to shake his head and splutter, "No, sir. No fire."

"No fire? Observe the smoke, boy. No smoke without fire, don't you know? And what is that appalling odoriferous emanation?"

"Beg pardon, sir?"

"The stink, boy. What is that dreadful stink?"

"Supper, sir. Chinese supper."

Mr Trump's face turned a bright shade of puce under his oil-slicked hair. To Sparrow, looking up at him, he seemed enormous, his tight black evening suit straining to cover his bulging belly. Catching sight of the little cooking stove, he pointed an accusing finger at it and let out a roar.

"What is that?" he demanded. "Are you not aware that the preparation of comestibles in the dressing rooms is in complete contravention of the regulations of this establishment?"

The Chinese men looked at him in blank bewilderment. Sparrow came to their rescue.

"He means it's against the rules to cook in the dressing room," he interpreted.

"That is what I expostulated," Mr Trump huffed.

Li translated for the men, who began to protest loudly in Chinese with much waving of hands and shaking of heads.

Mr Trump raised his voice to be heard above their clamour. "I am prepared to overlook the current infraction. But any further transgressions will result in a peremptory termination of your engagement." Then, while Sparrow was still trying to work out what this meant, he translated it himself. "Do it again and you're fired," he growled. "Now get this lot cleared up, and look sharp about it!"

The manager turned on his heel and marched away down the corridor, muttering to himself, "Chinese supper, indeed!"

Sparrow looked at Li and shrugged. "Everybody's dead scared of fire in the theatre," he said. "Can't be too careful, eh?"

The men looked unhappy but turned off the stove and began clearing up, grumbling glumly as they did so.

"Must eat," Li told Sparrow. "Need be strong for act. You see."

"I could always get you some cheese and ham rolls from the bar," Sparrow offered. "And a nice pickled onion, maybe?"

"Pickoo anya?" the boy said, puzzled.

"Pickled onion, yeah. They're quite spicy."

"OK. I try. You want more this?" He picked up another piece of meat from the pan. Sparrow held his hand in front of his mouth and backed away.

"No, ta. Not just now," he said hurriedly. The Chinese men burst out laughing, and Sparrow grinned back at them and dashed off.

For the rest of the evening Sparrow was kept busy fetching and carrying for the other artistes and changing the placards at the side of the stage that gave the number of each act. But he did manage to watch most of the Chinese acrobats' performance and was amazed at their skills as they juggled clubs and bottles and even swords, bent themselves into impossible shapes and leapt and bounded across the stage. His new young friend was in the middle of everything, being picked up and thrown about and caught in mid-air by the others. He finished by climbing nimbly up a human pyramid formed by the men and balancing on one hand, upside down, on the top man's head, bringing him a big round of well-deserved applause.

As he left the theatre after the show, Sparrow's head was filled with dreams of becoming an acrobat like Li. How long would it take to learn? he wondered. And could he ever be brave enough to be thrown about the stage like a rubber ball? Or to climb up a human pyramid like a monkey? Perhaps he would be better trying his hand at juggling, but he wasn't sure he could dare to do it with sharp, curved swords like the Chinese men did. He was so full of what he had seen that he was halfway home before he remembered about Lily and that he had promised to keep looking out for her.

Feeling guilty, he did not go straight home but turned into alleys and courts along the way. It was dark, of course, and the light from street lamps and the moon made the shadows in door-ways and corners seem even deeper. He was just about to give up when he stumbled over something lying on the ground behind a low wall. It must have been thrown there during the day. He picked it up and saw it was a tray like those the flower girls carried around their necks. In the dark he could just make out little bunches of flowers and buttonholes lying on the ground around it.

"I found somethin'! Somethin' important!" Sparrow yelled excitedly as he tumbled back into HQ.

He was surprised to see that none of the other Boys had gone to bed yet. Instead, they were all sitting around the candlelit cellar with worried faces.

"Look," he said. "Lily's flower tray."

He held it up for them to see, wondering why they did not seem more excited.

"Good lad," said Wiggins, reaching out and taking the tray. "Where was it?"

"In Clarke's Court. Behind a little wall. She must have chucked it there."

"What'd she want to do that for?" Beaver asked. "She won't be able to earn no money if she ain't got no flower tray. And if she can't earn no money…"

"Here," Queenie interrupted him, "let's have a look at that."

She took the tray from Wiggins and moved closer to the candle to examine it.

"This ain't Lily's tray," she said after inspecting it carefully. "It's Rosie's."

There was a gasp of horror from everyone.

"It can't be," said Sparrow. He looked around the room. "Where *is* Rosie?"

"She ain't come home yet," Queenie told him. "We been out lookin' for her, but we can't find her nowhere. Even asked PC Higgins to keep an eye out for her."

"Fat lot of good that'll do," Shiner said gloomily. "Clean vanished, she 'as."

"Somethin' must have happened to her," said Gertie. "She wouldn't have run away. Not our Rosie."

"That's what she said about Lily, ain't it?" Wiggins said, looking serious. "This needs some thinking about. You lot, go to bed and get some shut-eye while I try to work it out."

Wiggins spent the night curled up in his special armchair, which he always used when he had a problem to solve. To help him think, he put Mr Holmes's old deerstalker hat on his head, and from time to time he sucked on the curly pipe – empty, of course – while the others, especially Queenie, tossed and turned in their beds, restless with worry about Rosie. But by morning Wiggins was no closer to solving the mystery of why Lily and now Rosie had gone missing. He half hoped that Rosie would show up when it was time to set out for the market, but when she didn't, he decided to go to Covent Garden himself.

"What d'you want to go there for?" Queenie asked him. "It was round here that Rosie disappeared."

"Yeah, but don't you remember, she said somebody at the market told her about some of the other girls going missing."

"Oh yeah, so she did. Who was it told her now? I can't remember."

"I think she was called Lizzie or somethin'," Beaver piped up.

"Yeah, that's it," said Queenie. "Lizzie, I'm sure it was."

"Thanks, Beav," said Wiggins. "Come on – let's you and me go and find her."

"Can't I come?" asked Queenie.

"No. Best if you stay here in case Rosie comes home and needs looking after. And the rest of you keep searching for her, just in case."

The early morning crush of carts had cleared by the time Wiggins and Beaver arrived. Covent Garden was still busy, but now it was like an ordinary daytime market, with housewives and servants buying vegetables for that day's meals, and flowers for their houses. Most of the traffic was carriages and cabs, and delivery vans bringing groceries to the houses around the Piazza. Over in the far corner, two men in a green van from a Chinese laundry were collecting soiled sheets and towels from Hummum's Hotel.

Weaving their way out of the market were a few donkey carts driven by costermongers, who sold fruit and vegetables from them on the streets of London. On high days and holidays, when they wore their best clothes decorated all over with thousands of shiny pearl buttons, the costermongers – costers for short – were known as pearly kings and queens. But for now they were in their everyday clothes, with plain cloth caps set at a jaunty angle on their heads, and bright scarves knotted tightly around their necks. Wiggins spoke to one of them whose donkey was refusing to move.

"Having a spot of bother, mate?" Wiggins asked him.

"Bloomin' animal," the coster complained. "Gone on strike, she 'as. They says donkeys is stupid. 'Silly ass,' they say. They should try tellin' that to my Clara, 'ere."

"Why, what does she want?"

"I know exac'ly what she wants. An' she knows I know. Ain't that right, Clarabell?"

The donkey bared its teeth as though it was smiling. The coster sighed heavily and turned to Beaver.

"Pass me one o' them carrots, will you?"

Beaver chose the juiciest-looking carrot from the pile on the back of the cart.

"D'you want to give it 'er?" the man asked.

"Can I?"

"Yeah, but keep yer hand flat or she'll 'ave yer fingers off."

Beaver held out the carrot on the palm of his hand, and the donkey took it and chewed it noisily and with great enjoyment.

"Talk about eatin' up the profits," the coster said wryly. "I'll have nothin' left to sell by the time she's done." He looked back at Wiggins. "Don't recollect seein' you afore," he said. "What brings you round 'ere?"

"We're looking for a girl," Wiggins told him.

"Ain't we all!" the man replied, laughing. "Still, good-lookin' young blokes like you, shouldn't be too much trouble."

"No, no," Beaver corrected him, blushing bright red. "We're lookin' for one perticular girl."

"Name of Lizzie," said Wiggins. "Any idea where we might find her?"

"Lizzie?" The man pushed his cap back and

scratched his head. "No. Don't know nobody here called Lizzie."

"A flower girl," Wiggins said. "She's the top of all the girls. Been here for years."

The man's face cleared. "Oh, you don't mean Lizzie. You means *Liza*. Everybody knows Liza. Look, that's her – over there." And he pointed to the church, where the girl was sitting on the steps with a big basket of violets and other tiny blooms.

"That's right," said Eliza when they told her what the coster had said. "Everybody knows Liza – only it's Eliza, if you wanna get it right."

"Sorry," said Wiggins. "Eliza, then."

"That's better. More ladylike, don't you fink? D'you know, I had a posh toff round 'ere t'other day said 'e could turn me into a real lady if I let 'im learn me 'ow to talk proper."

"What did you say?" asked Beaver.

"Told 'im where he could get off, didn't I? I've 'eard 'baht geezers like that, ain't I?"

Wiggins and Beaver looked at each other, worried.

"D'you think that's what happened to Rosie?" Wiggins asked Eliza.

"Rosie?" she replied. "Why? Has somethin' happened to her?"

"She's disappeared, just like Lily."

Eliza looked shocked. She pursed her lips and let out a whistle.

"Crikey," she said. "That makes about 'alf a dozen gels gone missin'. There's Rosie and Lily, and then there's Poppy and Violet and Marigold and Daisy and … oh, lawks… There's somethin' terrible goin' on! What's 'appened to 'em all?"

THE VANISHING FLOWER GIRLS

"Wot we gonna do?" Beaver asked. "They can't have just vanished, can they? I mean, if they'd just disappeared, like somethin' in one of them conjurin' tricks, that'd be magic ... and if there really was magic, you could..."

"Magic? What's 'e on about?" asked Eliza.

"Never mind that," Wiggins told her. "You're right. There is something terrible going on. And we gotta do something about it."

Eliza stood up. She picked up her basket of flowers and handed it to a coster who was selling apples from a barrow near by. "Keep an eye on that for me, will you, Alfie?" she asked.

"Why? Where you off to?" the man replied.

"The cop shop."

"Cor blimey! You gonna turn yourself in?

What you been up to, then?"

"Nothin' to do with you," she laughed. "Come on, lads."

"Where we goin'?" Beaver asked, puzzled.

"I just said, didn't I? The police station. We got the biggest in London just round the corner."

She led the two boys across the Piazza, narrowly avoiding being knocked down by the laundry van that had just left the hotel. They made their way through the Floral Hall and out into Bow Street, alongside the tall white pillars of the Opera House.

"There," said Eliza, pointing across the street to an imposing new building made of grey stone. "Bow Street nick."

They crossed the road and climbed the steps to the grand entrance, pushing their way in through the big swing doors. Eliza seemed to know her way about, and Wiggins and Beaver were happy to follow her.

"You been here afore?" Wiggins asked her.

"A few times," she said with a grin. "Collectin' my old man after 'e's been brought in for 'avin' a few too many."

"A few too many what?" Beaver asked.

"Drinks, of course. He don't get too much of nothin' else, that's for sure." And she laughed as she approached the tall counter, its polished wood gleaming as it reflected the modern electric lights hanging from the high ceiling. The sergeant behind the counter gave her a smile that lit up his round, red face and raised the corners of his heavy moustache.

"Now then, Eliza," he greeted her. "We ain't got him here. Not today."

"No, I know you 'aven't. That ain't why I'm 'ere."

"What's up, then?"

Eliza told the sergeant all about the missing flower girls. He listened carefully, then thought for a moment, tapping a pencil against his teeth.

"So," he said, "these girls have gone missing, eh? What makes you think they haven't just run away?"

"'Cos one of 'em is our friend Rosie," Wiggins said. "And she wouldn't."

"Oh, and who might you be?"

"My name's Wiggins. Arnold Wiggins."

"Oh, yes?"

"And I'm Beaver. We're the Baker Street Boys. Well, two of 'em. There's another five of us altogether – or at least there was till Rosie vanished. So you see, we need to find her, 'cos…"

"Whoa, whoa! Steady on, now." The sergeant held up a big hand as though stopping traffic in the street. "What do you think might have happened to these girls? D'you think they've been murdered? Has anybody found any bodies?"

Beaver swallowed hard and went very pale at the thought. Wiggins shook his head.

"No," he said. "No bodies. But we think they might have been kidnapped."

"That's right," said Eliza. "Somebody might have 'em all locked up somewhere."

"Kidnapped?" the sergeant asked. "Who'd want to kidnap a bunch of flower girls? Who'd pay a ransom for them?"

Wiggins shrugged hopelessly. What the sergeant said was true. Villains kidnapped people for money, and none of the girls knew anyone who had any.

"No ransom demands. No bodies," the sergeant

went on. "As far as we know, there's been no crime committed. So I'm sorry, Eliza my love, but it's not a police matter. I'll tell my constables on the beat to keep their eyes open for any sign of the missing girls, but that's all I can do for now."

The three youngsters thanked him and headed disconsolately for the door. As they reached it, the sergeant called out to them.

"Wait a minute. Baker Street Boys, did you say? Are you the young scamps that help Mr Sherlock Holmes with his investigations?"

"That's right," Wiggins told him. "That's us."

"Well then, you want to get Mr Holmes on the case. This isn't a crime, it's a mystery. Just the thing for him, I'd have thought."

The three youngsters stood on the pavement outside the police station. Eliza said she would spread the word among all the market people and get them to look out for the girls. Wiggins agreed that that was a good idea. But he believed Mr Holmes was the only person who could find the answer to the mystery and he said he would go straight back to Baker Street to see him. As they walked back past the market, deep in thought, Beaver suddenly grabbed his arm.

"Wiggins! Look!" he gasped. He pointed to a black carriage standing on the corner of the street. It had a small monogram painted on the door – a curly letter "M". As they watched, it moved off, round the corner and out of sight.

"Moriarty!" Wiggins exclaimed. "I might have knowed."

"Who's Moriarty?" Eliza wanted to know.

"The biggest crook in London," Wiggins told her. "The mastermind of crime."

"You think 'e's got somethin' to do wiv all this?"

"I dunno. That's what we gotta find out."

Back in Baker Street, Wiggins and Beaver hurried straight to number 221b to find Mr Holmes. When they tugged at the shiny brass bell-pull, the door was opened as usual by Billy, Mrs Hudson's pageboy. But for once he did not greet them with a snooty sneer. Instead, he seemed quite subdued and his face and eyes were red, as though he had been crying.

"Hello," said Wiggins. "What's up?"

"Nothing," Billy replied.

"Come on," Wiggins continued. "You can tell us. We're your friends."

Billy looked surprised. He had never thought of the Boys as his friends. In fact, he did not have any real friends and Wiggins's words made him feel like crying again.

"Are you?" he asked. "D'you really mean it?"

"Course I do, me old china."

"China?" Billy said sharply. "What d'you mean by that?"

"The old rhyming slang, you know? China plate – mate."

"Oh, yeah. Of course. I thought you was talking about…"

He stopped and bit his lip.

"What?"

"That's what I'm in trouble over. Somebody's pinched one of Mrs Hudson's ornaments, and she blames me."

"What, she thinks you took it?"

"No, but it's my job to open the door and let people in and out."

"And keep an eye on them, like you do with us?" Wiggins grinned.

Billy nodded miserably. "But I told her, there's only been the usual tradesmen in this morning. I know 'em all. And they wouldn't have pinched it."

"What was it like, this ornament?"

"It was a little statue. Carved out of jade."

"What's jade?" Beaver asked.

"It's a sort of stone, green and shiny. It stood on the hall table there."

"Oh, I remember it," said Wiggins. "Like a funny animal. Right?"

"That's right. A dragon. Cost a lot of money, Mrs Hudson says. Came all the way from China."

"Oh, I see. Well, I'm sorry, Billy. Any other time we'd love to help you track it down. But we're a bit busy just now. You oughta tell Mr Holmes."

"I would. But he's not here."

Wiggins and Beaver looked at each other in dismay. They had been relying on Mr Holmes to solve the mystery of the missing flower girls and help them to find Rosie.

"What about Dr Watson, then?"

"He's gone with him. So you can't see either of them, if that's what you came for. Sorry."

As they all gathered back in HQ, the other Boys were gloomy when Wiggins and Beaver told them what had happened.

"Well," said Queenie. "If Mr Holmes has gone off somewhere and the coppers don't wanna know, it's up to us to find Rosie, ain't it?"

"But we already looked everywhere," grumbled Shiner. "Ain't nowhere left to look."

"There's gotta be," Wiggins said. "We thought we'd looked everywhere yesterday, but Sparrow managed to find her tray, didn't he?"

"And a fat lot of good it did us. We ain't never gonna find 'er."

"Oi! That's enough of that," Queenie scolded her younger brother. "'Never' is a big word. We don't want no defeatist talk."

"What's that supposed to mean?"

"It means," said Wiggins, "saying we ain't gonna win. If that's what we think, we never will. So we're gonna get out there and look again. Right?"

"Right," chorused the others.

"Where shall we start?" asked Gertie.

Wiggins headed for the door. "Sparrow," he said, "I want you to show me exac'ly where you found that tray."

Sparrow led the Boys through the streets to Clarke's Court. When they arrived, he pointed to the low wall.

"It was behind there," he said.

Wiggins waved his hand at the others to tell them to stand back while he examined the scene, looking around with care for any footprints or other evidence. He reached into his coat pocket and pulled out the old magnifying glass that Mr Holmes had given him. Bending down, he peered through it to examine the pavement for clues. When he was satisfied that there was nothing, he moved to the wall and looked over it.

"Oh, my word!" he exclaimed. "That settles it."

The ground on the other side of the wall was scattered with small bunches of flowers and buttonholes.

"Was these here last night?" he asked Sparrow.

"I think so. Couldn't see much, it was too dark. I only found the tray 'cos I tripped over it. I didn't know it was Rosie's."

"Those are Rosie's flowers," said Queenie. "What she made up yesterday morning. Look, they're done up in her special way."

Wiggins stared at the flowers, hoping they could tell him something, offer him some sort of clue. Then he had an idea.

"How many d'you think she'd sold," he asked, "if these are what she had left?"

Queenie scratched her head, trying to remember how many little bunches she had seen Rosie tying up and arranging on her tray.

"'Bout half her stock," she said. "Why?"

"Well," Wiggins said. "If she'd sold about half her stock, that probably means it was halfway through the day when she stopped."

The others gazed at him in awe.

"That's real clever," said Beaver. "I'd never have thought of that."

"Yeah, but what good is it?" Shiner wanted to know.

"Well," Wiggins replied. "It means if somebody kidnapped her, they must have done it in broad daylight."

"But if they did," Queenie puzzled, "how could they have took her away without everybody in the street seein' what they was doin'?"

"That's a very good question. And when we've found the answer, we'll be halfway to finding Rosie."

CHASING A DRAGON

"Cheer up, lad! You look like you've lost a quid and found a tanner," Bert the stage doorkeeper at the Imperial Music Hall greeted Sparrow when he arrived for work that evening.

If he *had* lost a pound and found a sixpence, as Bert said, Sparrow might have been able to cheer up. But worrying about Rosie, he couldn't manage even the faintest of smiles.

"I ain't lost a quid," he told Bert. "I've lost a friend."

Bert listened with sympathy as Sparrow told him about Rosie, and he promised he would tell everybody he knew to look out for her as well as Lily and the other missing girls. But as he handed him his jacket, he reminded him to try and put on a brave face while he was at work. Mr Trump wouldn't be as understanding, and he wouldn't put up with a miserable call boy in his theatre.

Sparrow did his best not to look too miserable, and managed quite well for most of the show. But when a pretty young woman called Little Lottie Lupin went on stage at the end of the first half to sing a popular old song called "Won't You Buy My Pretty Flowers", it was too much for him to bear. Dressed as a flower girl and carrying a tray of paper blossoms, Little Lottie sang very sweetly:

"Underneath the lamplight's glitter
Stands a little fragile girl,
Heedless of the cold wind bitter,
As it round about her twirls.
While the hundreds pass unheeding
In the evening's waning hours,
Still she cries with tearful pleading,
'Won't you buy my pretty flowers?'
There are many sad and dreary
In this pleasant world of ours
Crying every night so bitter,
'Won't you buy my pretty flowers?'"

Sparrow couldn't stop a tear rolling down his cheek. He was still sniffing when he knocked on the door of the Chinese acrobats' dressing room to give them their call to go on stage. They were very concerned to see him looking so upset.

"Why you sad?" Li, his young Chinese friend, asked him.

Sparrow began to tell them about Rosie, and the other girls, and how he was sure they had been kidnapped. But before he could say any more, Mr Trump came along the corridor and glared at him.

"Come along, lad," the manager said. "No time for protracted palavers. Get the next numbers up and look sharp about it!"

The acrobats completed their performance to their usual loud applause. As they came off the stage and headed back to their dressing room, one of the men hung back and plucked at Sparrow's sleeve. Drawing him into a dark corner, he looked around nervously then whispered in his ear.

"You want find friend," he said in broken

English, "you go look chasing dragon."

"Dragon?" Sparrow asked. "You mean, with scales and claws and wings and stuff?"

"Shh," the man hushed him. "Yes. Chasing dragon. By basin. Find you friend there."

Before he could say more, one of the other men appeared, grabbed him by the arm and pulled him away, muttering angrily at him in Chinese. Sparrow repeated the words to himself, trying to make some sense out of them. But they meant nothing to him. He repeated them again, to make sure he would remember exactly what the man had said, then hurried off to call the next act before Mr Trump came after him.

When the show was finished, Sparrow could hardly wait to get back to HQ to tell the other Boys what the Chinese man had said.

"Listen! You gotta listen!" he shouted as he ran down the steps and burst into the cellar. "I got a clue! A real clue!"

The others were weary and depressed after a long day of searching the streets. They were all feeling edgy and quarrelsome – Queenie nearly boxed Shiner's ears for saying it was all a waste of time, till Beaver stopped her – but they perked up when Sparrow arrived, bringing new hope.

"Come on, then. Spit it out," said Queenie.

"A dragon. We gotta look for a dragon," Sparrow blurted out. "And a bowl of somethin'."

The rest of the Boys stared at him, open-mouthed.

"You mean like a dragon what breathes fire and smoke?" asked Beaver.

"What you talkin' about?" Shiner scoffed. "Ain't no such things as dragons."

"How do you know?" demanded Gertie. "You never heard of St George?"

"That was in the olden days. They was all killed off years ago."

"Ah, but what if one had escaped and hid up in a cavern somewhere?" Beaver said, looking worried. "It could have survived, and if it had, then…"

"Quiet, all of you!" shouted Wiggins, rising from his special chair, where he had been trying to think. "Now, Sparrow, calm down and tell me exac'ly what you're on about."

Sparrow took a deep breath and tried to speak

calmly. "There's this Chinaman," he began.

"Where was this?"

"At the theatre. One of the acrobats in the show. Dead good, they are, you oughta see 'em…"

"Sparrow!"

"They knows as we're lookin' for Rosie, 'cos I told Li, and the others was there."

"So what happened?"

"Well, after they'd finished their act, when they come off stage, one of the geezers comes to me and whispers, all secret, like he didn't want the rest of 'em to hear, 'You want find friend, you go look chasing dragon.'"

"What you talkin' in that funny voice for?" Shiner asked.

"'Cos that's the way they talk. All Chinamen talk like that…"

"Never mind that," Wiggins said. "Just tell us what exac'ly he said."

"Well, like I say, he says if we want to find Rosie we gotta chase after the dragon."

"You sure he didn't mean a dragonfly?" Queenie asked. "I seen dragonflies flittin' about.

They look fierce but they're harmless really."

"No. I asked him if he meant a dragon, wiv scales and claws and wings an' all that. And he says yes."

"That's all he said?" Wiggins scratched his head. "He never said where this dragon was?"

"No. Only that it's by a bowl or somethin'."

"What sort of a bowl?"

"P'raps it's what the dragon eats his dinner off," suggested Shiner. "P'raps he cooks his victims first wiv his hot breath and then…"

"Shiner!" Beaver and Queenie shouted together.

"And that's all he said?" asked Wiggins.

"Yeah. That's all. We gotta chase after the dragon if we want to find Rosie. Then one of the other Chinamen come and grabbed him and took him off, afore he could say any more. Like they didn't want him tellin' me nothin'."

The Boys were stunned into silence at the thought of having to fight a dragon to rescue Rosie. They imagined themselves braving its fiery breath and sharp claws, and shuddered with fear.

"You need armour, and a horse and a lance to

fight dragons," Beaver mused. "Where we gonna find all that? I mean, if it's got a cave and it's got Rosie and Lily and the rest of the girls shut up inside, it'll be guarding the entrance and we'll have to get past it, and…"

"Beaver!" Queenie shouted. "Stop it! You're givin' everybody the heebie-jeebies."

"I'm not scared of no old dragon," Gertie asserted boldly.

"Nor me," Shiner joined in.

"I'd biff him on the nose, so I would," said Gertie, holding up a fist. "Soon show him who's boss!"

A new, even more awful thought struck Beaver. "But what if there's more than one?" he asked. "What if there's a whole den of dragons, all waitin'…"

"Beaver!" Wiggins yelled. "I told you – ain't no such thing as dragons."

"But what if there was?" asked Shiner. "What if somebody had one, and they had to feed it wiv maidens? Like the monster in that story you used to read to me, sis, afore Mum died. You remember?"

Queenie nodded. "That was the minotaur in Ancient Greece," she said. "Lived in the labyrinth."

"The what?" asked Gertie.

"The labyrinth. It was sort of a underground maze. Like a giant puzzle. Once you got in, you couldn't never find your way out again."

"And the monster lived in the middle, didn't he?" Shiner recalled. "And got fed with boys and gels…"

They all looked at each other, their faces pale and white in the candlelight, as they all thought the same thing, even Wiggins. Could there be a secret monster living somewhere deep under London? In the sewers, maybe? Everyone knew that the sewers were like a labyrinth, where you could easily get lost, and that there were thousands of rats living in them. But who knew what else might be living down there?

After what seemed like a long time, Wiggins cleared his throat noisily.

"We ain't gonna solve nothing tonight," he announced. "You lot, off to bed, while I put my thinking cap on. And no nightmares. Remember, there's no such things as dragons… Not really."

* * *

In spite of what Wiggins had said, most of the Boys did dream of dragons. And most of them called out in their sleep from time to time during the night, while he dozed in his chair, sucking on his empty pipe. He wished Mr Holmes was around – he was sure the great detective would be able to make sense out of everything and would tell him what to do. Even Dr Watson might be able to offer him some advice. But without either of them it was down to him.

By morning, Wiggins was still no nearer to solving the mystery, but he had had one bright idea. "If there is a dragon in London," he told the Boys as they sat around the big table eating their stale bread, "there's one place it's most likely to be."

"In the circus?" suggested Sparrow.

"Good try," said Wiggins, "but that's not what I'm thinking of."

"Swimmin' in the river," said Beaver. "Where the sewers come out."

"No. Nor that, neither."

The others waited impatiently until he told

them with a note of triumph in his voice: "The zoo."

They all stared at Wiggins with wide-eyed admiration. He had done it again.

"And if they ain't got one," he went on, "they're sure to know where to find one."

"Well, what are we waitin' for?" asked Queenie. "Let's go."

London Zoo was in Regent's Park, not far from HQ. The Boys hurried up Baker Street and then into the park, which seemed like a different world from the one they knew. People strolled along the broad paths without a care in the world. An elderly gentleman in a top hat leant on his silver-tipped cane, puffing at a cigar as he watched the gardeners tending the flower-beds and borders. Nursemaids pushed babies in shiny prams and chatted to each other while the young children in their care played happily on the grass under their watchful eyes. It was hard to imagine that somewhere near by a villain, or a gang of villains, was snatching flower girls from the street. It was even harder to imagine a fiery dragon in such surroundings.

"Stop!" A large park policeman blocked their way. "What are you lot up to?" he demanded.

"We ain't up to nothin'," Queenie replied.

"You'd better not be. This here is a royal park, you know."

"You mean it belongs to Her Majesty?" asked Beaver.

"It does. So don't even think about getting up to any mischief."

"We don't get up to mischief," Wiggins told him. "We're the Baker Street Boys."

"And we assist Mr Sherlock Holmes with his investigations," Sparrow added, sounding a bit like Mr Trump with his long words.

The policeman sucked his teeth thoughtfully. "Do you, indeed. And what investigations are you assisting him with at the moment?"

"At the moment," Beaver said, "Mr Holmes is away. But if he wasn't then we'd be assisting him in trying to rescue our friend Rosie, what's disappeared along wiv a lot of other flower girls."

"That sounds serious," the policeman said, pulling his notebook and pencil out of his pocket. He licked the end of the pencil. "Have you reported it?"

"Yes," Queenie answered. "We told the sergeant at Bow Street police station."

"Bow Street, eh? Well you can't do any better than that. What did the sergeant say?"

"That it ain't a police matter, 'cos we ain't found no bodies."

"I see. Well, in that case..." The policeman closed his notebook and put it back in his pocket. "Sounds like a job for your friend Mr Sherlock Holmes," he said.

"But Mr Holmes is away," said Wiggins, "so we gotta investigate for ourselves."

"In the park?" asked the policeman. "I don't think they're anywhere in the park. We'd have seen 'em. Anyway, we don't allow flower sellers in the park."

"We ain't lookin' for 'em in the park," said Queenie. "We're lookin' for a dragon."

The policeman smiled. "We don't allow dragons in the park, neither."

"We know that," said Wiggins. "We're going to the zoo."

"I shouldn't think they allow dragons in there either. They might eat all the other animals. Not to mention the keepers." He chuckled loudly, pleased with his little joke. "What's a dragon got to do with your missing flower girls?" he asked.

"We was told we'd find 'em if we chased after the dragon."

"And who told you that?"

"A Chinaman," said Sparrow.

The policeman threw back his head and laughed. "All right," he said. "You've had your fun. Now off you go. The zoo's that way."

"We're not having fun," Sparrow told him, on the verge of tears. "It's true!"

"Course it is. And I'm Jack the Ripper. Now get off with you." He watched them walking miserably away, then called after them, "And don't worry – if I spot any Chinese dragons lurking in the bushes, I'll be sure to let you know."

As the Boys approached the entrance to the zoo, they heard an animal roaring ferociously from behind the railings. They gulped and looked at each other nervously.

"D'you think that could be one?" Shiner asked.

"Dunno," said Beaver. "Sounds fierce enough, don't it?"

Suddenly, the idea of fighting a dragon did not seem so attractive. But the gatekeeper was already looking down at them from his glass box beside the turnstile; there was no going back.

"No admittance for unaccompanied juveniles," he declared sternly.

"What's that mean?" Gertie asked.

"Means we can't go in without a grown-up," Wiggins replied.

"And in any case it would be sixpence each," the man continued. "Have you got any money?"

"We don't want to go in to look at the animals," Wiggins said. "We wants to talk to somebody. It's important."

"Matter of life and death," Beaver added.

"What about?"

"Dragons," said Wiggins.

"Ain't no such thing. Leastwise, there ain't been for hundreds of years."

"Are you sure?"

"If there was, we'd have one. And we haven't.

We've got plenty of lizards and iguanas and stuff. But definitely no dragons."

"So you don't know where we might find one?"

The man laughed. "In a fairy tale, maybe. Now go on, hop it – and stop wasting my time."

The Boys trailed slowly back through the streets towards HQ. No one would give them any help in finding Rosie and the other girls, and most people didn't even take them seriously. Mr Holmes and Dr Watson were both away, so they were no use. Even Wiggins was starting to think their search was hopeless. But suddenly Beaver spotted something.

"Look!" he shouted. "Look there!"

He pointed a finger trembling with excitement. There, bowling along the street, was a green van, pulled by a shiny black horse. Driving it was a Chinese man dressed in a blue cotton top and baggy trousers, with a long pigtail hanging down his back. Another Chinese man sat beside him. But Beaver was not pointing at the two men. He was pointing at the sign painted on the side of the van. "THE LIMEHOUSE LAUN-DRY," it read, and underneath was a picture of a strange creature with flames coming out of its mouth.

"Look!" Beaver said again. "A dragon!"

FOLLOW THAT VAN!

The Boys stared at the green van as it moved away down the street. Could this be the dragon they had to chase? After all, there were Chinamen driving the van, and it had been a Chinaman who had told Sparrow.

"What's it say?" asked Gertie.

"The Limehouse Laundry," Shiner read out slowly. "What's a limehouse?"

"It ain't a thing," Wiggins told him. "It's a place. Down the river in the East End, where all the docks are."

"D'you think that's where they're goin'?" Sparrow asked.

"Dunno. We'll have to follow 'em and see. Come on."

The van was travelling quite quickly, and

they had to run to catch up with it.

"Don't get too close," Wiggins called out. "We don't want 'em to see us."

Queenie and Beaver, who couldn't run as fast as the others, were soon out of breath and fell back. Although they were puffing and panting, they gritted their teeth and kept on, determined not to get left behind even while the gap was getting bigger. Then Queenie felt a sharp pain in her side which almost forced her to stop.

"Oh, Beav," she groaned, "I got a stitch."

"Try to keep goin'," he told her. "See if you can run it off."

Queenie nodded speechlessly – she didn't have enough breath to talk. But she found enough to let out a little scream when a large brown dog charged out of a house, barking furiously. She had always been scared of dogs, ever since one had bitten her hand when she was quite small, and she was terrified of this one as it snapped and snarled at her heels through bared yellow fangs. Looking back at it instead of where she was going, she tripped and fell into the gutter. The dog leapt at her and would have sunk its teeth into her leg, but Beaver bravely came to the rescue, knocking it off her and driving it away. When he turned back to her, he saw she was starting to cry – which was worrying, because Queenie never cried.

"You all right?" he asked. "Did it bite you?"

"No, it ain't that," she replied. "We've lost 'em. We'll never catch up with 'em now."

"Never mind," he said. "Are you all right?"

"We need to stick together if we're gonna find out what's happened to Rosie."

"I know. But can you walk?"

"Dunno. I've twisted my ankle pretty bad, and my knee hurts somethin' rotten."

"Best thing we can do now is get you back home. We can wait there for Wiggins and the others."

He helped her to her feet and tried to make sure she hadn't broken any bones. Although she desperately wanted to go on searching for Rosie, Queenie knew that Beaver was right.

"Thanks, Beav," she said, drying her eyes. "You're a brick. I thought I was a goner when that dog went for me."

"'S'all right," he said sheepishly. "Come on, you can lean on me. I'll be your crutch." And they set off together, to hobble back to HQ.

Wiggins, Sparrow, Shiner and Gertie followed the van until it stopped outside a big house. Then they dived into the shelter of a gateway further down the street and watched as the two men clambered down from their seat, walked round to the back and opened the rear door. The long pigtails hanging down their backs swung from side to side as they reached into the van and pulled out a large wicker basket with a closed lid. Wiggins had always thought that Chinese men were small, but these two were big and tough. Although the basket was obviously heavy, they lifted it easily and carried it between them up to the house.

"What d'you think's in that basket?" Gertie whispered.

"Dunno, but it's big enough to hold a body," Wiggins replied. "Or even two."

"There's some more in the back of the van," said Shiner. "I'm gonna look inside." And he darted forward and climbed in through the open door.

The others followed cautiously, keeping their eyes on the two men, who had now reached the side door of the house. Shiner was looking at the baskets and bundles of laundry in the back of the van.

"What can you see?" Wiggins asked him.

"Just a lot of washing and stuff. Ain't no girls in here."

"Right. Come out now."

"Wait a minute. What's this?"

Shiner had reached the end of the van and spotted something lying in a corner. He reached down and picked it up.

"Look at this!" he cried, holding it up for the others to see. It was a little bunch of flowers, a nosegay.

"That's one of Rosie's!" Gertie exclaimed. "I'll swear it's one of Rosie's."

They all stared open-mouthed at the little wilted flowers. None of them noticed the two men coming back until they heard a loud shout.

"Hey! You! What you do?"

The men were charging at them, waving their fists angrily.

"Wiggins! Watch out!" yelled Sparrow.

"Run for it!" Wiggins shouted. "Quick!"

Sparrow, Gertie and Wiggins took to their heels, and the three of them raced away down the street. In the van, Shiner realized there was no way he could get out before the men arrived. He ducked down and hid as they rushed out of the house gate and chased after the others – but not before one of them had slammed the van door shut.

The other three Boys raced along the street, the two Chinamen not far behind. They turned into a side street, and then another, hoping to lose their pursuers, but the men were still following.

"Quick! This way," Wiggins panted.

They turned another corner and found themselves facing a broad waterway – Regent's Canal. There was no bridge near by, no way of crossing it and nowhere to hide.

"Oh, crikey – they'll catch us now, for sure," cried Sparrow, looking around in despair.

"They don't have to," said Gertie. "Look."

A barge was passing along the canal, steered by a ruddy-faced man with a stubbly beard and bright, twinkling eyes under the peak of his dark brown cap. The boat was pulled by a powerful horse that plodded peacefully along the towpath, led by a girl who was about the same age as Wiggins, wearing a white cotton bonnet and a long pinafore over a pair of stout boots.

"Help! Hide us, please!" Gertie called out to them.

Without waiting to ask what was happening, the girl jerked her thumb at the boat. "Jump aboard," she said.

There was a gap of a few feet between the boat and the bank. Gertie leapt across it fearlessly, but Sparrow and Wiggins looked nervously down at the water. It seemed very deep.

"Hey up!" the boatman called with a grin. "Wot you more frit of? A drop o' water or them as is arter you?"

The two lads took a deep breath and jumped, landing safely on the little deck.

"That's the ticket," the man said. "Get in there

now and keep your heads down."

He pushed them down a step and through two narrow doors, which he closed behind them just as the two Chinamen came running round the corner. As the men skidded to a stop, looking about them for any sign of the Boys, the boatman took a stubby white clay pipe from the pocket of his corduroy jacket and gave them a cheery wave with it. Then he jammed the pipe between his teeth, struck a match on the seat of his trousers, and lit the black tobacco. Puffing happily, he left a trail of foul-smelling blue smoke hanging in the air as the boat continued on its way. Behind it, the two Chinamen hunted up and down the empty street, scratching their heads in puzzlement.

From the back of the green van, Shiner listened very carefully for any sound from the men. Hearing nothing, he decided it must be safe for him to make his escape. The van had no windows and it was so dark inside that he couldn't see anything. He had to feel his way to the doors, taking care not to make a noise just in case the men were near by. But when he reached the doors, he couldn't find a handle: there was no way of opening them from the inside. He was trapped.

Shiner sat down on the floor and thought very hard. If he shouted loudly, and maybe banged on the side of the van, then someone passing by in the street might hear him and let him out. But if the men were there, they would hear – and who knew what they might do to him? Still clutching the little flowers, he wondered what they had done to Rosie and the others. With a shiver of fear, he decided the best thing he could do was to go on hiding behind the baskets and bundles until the men came back and needed to open the doors. Then when they turned their backs or went away, he would be able to dive out and make a run for it. Carefully, he felt his way back to the corner and settled down to wait.

"All right, me ducks, yow can come out now," the boatman said, swinging the two little doors open. "They'm gone."

Wiggins, Gertie and Sparrow climbed out of

the snug little cabin where they had been hiding and thanked the man for saving them.

"Wot yow bin up to, then?" he asked, in his strange sing-song accent.

"We ain't bin up to nothing," Wiggins told him.

"So them Chinese chaps was after yow for nothing, was they?"

"It ain't what *we've* done," said Sparrow. "It's what *they've* done."

"Oh, yeah? And what would that be?"

"They've kidnapped our friend Rosie and a whole lot of other girls," Gertie told him.

"Kidnapped?" The boatman whistled. "That's serious, that is. What they done with 'em?"

"We don't know yet. That's what we're trying to find out," said Wiggins.

"Have yow told the coppers?"

"We've tried. But they don't believe us," said Sparrow.

The man nodded. "They never do," he said with feeling, and puffed hard on his pipe, creating clouds of smoke that made the Boys cough and their eyes water. Leaning on the big tiller that worked the rudder, he steered the barge into the bank.

"Oi, Nell!" he called and beckoned to the girl leading the horse. She had already slowed it down and now she stopped it and walked back to the boat.

"Am yow all right now?" she asked in the same accent as the man's.

"This is my little wench, Nelly," the man said. "And I'm Enoch."

The Boys introduced themselves, and Wiggins thanked Nelly for her help. "I don't know what they'd have done if they'd caught us," he told her.

"Slit your throats and chucked yow in the cut, most likely," she said with a cheerful grin.

"The cut?" asked Sparrow.

"Ar, yow know – the cut." She pointed to the water.

"The canal," Enoch explained. "That's what we call it – the cut."

"I dain't loike the look o' them two," Nelly went on. "Why was they after yow?"

Wiggins explained about Rosie and the other

missing flower girls, and Sparrow told them what the Chinese acrobat had said about having to chase a dragon if they wanted to find them.

"Phew!" Enoch let out a little whistle. "Sounds like a tall order if yow ask me," he said.

"What's that mean?" asked Gertie.

"Means it's very hard to do," said Wiggins. "Which we've already found out."

Nelly's eyes grew as big as saucers. "Are there really dragons nowadays?"

"Not as I've ever heard of," her father replied.

"That's what everybody told us," Wiggins went on. "Even at the zoo. Then we see this van…"

"With a picture of a dragon on the side," added Gertie.

"So we followed it," said Sparrow, "and when the Chinamen opened it up and was delivering stuff, we nipped in and looked in the back…"

"And our friend Shiner found one of Rosie's little bunches of flowers."

"But then the men come back and seen us. And they was mad."

"So yow had to run for it?" asked Nelly.

"We had to run for our lives," said Gertie.

"'Cos they knew we were on to 'em," Wiggins added.

"Right. But you got the flowers?" Enoch wanted to know.

"Shiner's got 'em."

"And where's Shiner?"

"Dunno. Run the other way – I hope."

Enoch took his pipe from his mouth and tapped out the burnt tobacco into the canal while he thought.

"What are you going to do now?" he asked.

"Well, there was a name on the van, under the dragon. The Limehouse Laundry."

"Limehouse, eh? That where you want to go?"

"Yes. If we can find how to get there…"

"Yow already have, lad."

"What d'you mean?"

"I mean that's where we'm going. This canal runs round London and ends up in the docks. At the Limehouse Basin."

"That's it!" Sparrow yelled, startling everyone. "That's what the acrobat said. It weren't a bowl, it was a basin – we have to chase the dragon by the basin, he said!"

Wiggins and Gertie stared at him in delight. Now they knew they were on the right track.

Sitting in the darkness in the back of the laundry van, Shiner heard the two men coming back, talking to each other in Chinese. He had no idea what they were saying, of course, but they did not sound happy, and seemed to be arguing. He felt the van sway as they climbed back up to the driving seat and heard the crack of the whip as they started the horse. The van picked up speed, bumping and rattling over the cobblestones, and he had to hang on tightly to stop himself being thrown about. Wherever the men were going, they were obviously in a hurry. And, like it or not, Shiner was going with them.

BY NARROWBOAT TO CHINATOWN

Enoch told Wiggins, Sparrow and Gertie that if they stayed on the boat with him and Nelly, he would take them to Limehouse, where they could carry on searching for Rosie and the other girls.

"There's a lot of Chinese living there," he told them. "As a matter of fact, people call it China-town, there's so many of 'em. They come off the ships, yow see."

"Have you ever sailed to China, Enoch?" Sparrow asked.

"China?" Enoch laughed. "No, my lad. I've spent my whole life on the cut."

"In this barge?"

"We don't call it a barge, son. It's a narrow-boat. Built special for the cut. No good for the sea, but we can go all over England on the cut. There's canals all over the country, and they'm all linked up. We've just carried a load of coal down the Grand Union from Brummagem."

"Brummagem? Where's that?"

"It's what yow Cockneys call Birmingham."

"I've heard of Birmingham," said Gertie. "Is that where you come from?"

"This is where I come from," said Enoch, nodding at the boat and the canal. "This is my home. I was born on a narrowboat like this, and married on one."

"Where's your wife now?" asked Wiggins.

"Sad to say, her died a couple o' years back, God rest her. So now it's just me and my little Nell. Her's a good wench, is Nelly. Takes care of me and looks after the boat, just like her mam. What do yow think of our *Betsy*, then?"

The Boys looked around, puzzled, then saw the name, *Betsy*, painted on the side of the cabin in ornate yellow lettering. Around it, every inch of woodwork was covered with beautiful paintings of roses and castles and geometric patterns, all in bright colours. Even the water can standing on top of the cabin was painted all over with flowers, and so was the chimney pipe that poked through the roof carrying smoke from the shiny black coal stove in the corner of the cabin. The big, red-painted tiller was decorated with sparkling white rope, plaited and knotted into intricate shapes. The cosy cabin, fitted with built-in cupboards and fold-away furniture, had white lace curtains over the window and pretty plates propped up on narrow ledges along the walls. Even though they were carrying a cargo of coal, everything was spotlessly clean.

"It's beautiful," said Sparrow. "I'd love to live on a boat like this."

"The cabin's just like the inside of our old van," Gertie said. "Very snug." And she told Enoch how she used to live in a caravan with her father, clip-clopping through the country lanes between the villages where he used to mend people's pots and pans. Thinking of it made her sad, and she stood up quickly, before the tears could come.

"Can I go and walk with Nelly and the horse?" she asked. "I love horses."

"Course you can," said Enoch. "Her'll be glad of a bit of company."

"Keep your eyes open, though," Wiggins warned. "In case those two come back."

Queenie's ankle was very painful. She could only bear to walk on it by leaning on Beaver's shoulder – he offered to give her a piggyback ride, but she said she could manage. Walking very slowly, they finally got home to HQ, where Beaver sat her down in Wiggins's special chair and fetched a bowl of water to bathe her grazed knee. Then he found a piece of rag in the clothes chest, tore it into a strip and bound up her ankle.

"It's swelled up a bit, but it don't look too bad," he told her.

"Thanks. I s'pose it could have been worse."

"Yeah," he said. "If that dog had got his teeth into you, I don't know what we'd have done. I've heard tell as how if a mad dog bites you, you go mad and foam at the mouth and all that and start bitin' other people and then they go mad as well, and then…"

"Ta very much, Beaver," Queenie said, cutting

him short. "I don't want to know about that."

"Oh. No. Sorry."

"All I want to know is, what's happened to Rosie, and where's Wiggins and the others?"

Gertie was enjoying walking along the towpath with Nelly and Clover the horse, a lovely chestnut mare with a long black mane and big hooves covered in floppy white hair. Clover was towing the *Betsy* with a long white rope attached to a harness behind her. Looking at the size of the boat and the amount of coal piled up under the black tarpaulin, Gertie said it was amazing that one horse could pull such a heavy load.

"That's 'cos it's floating on the water," said Nelly. "Once it's started, it's easy to keep it moving – and it's all on the level. Water don't run uphill." .

"How do you get over hills, then?"

"You don't. You either climb over 'em with locks, like going up stairs, or you go under 'em through tunnels. Like this one coming up."

Looking ahead, Gertie could see they were approaching a hill. The banks of the canal were getting higher on either side as they entered a cutting, and at the end of it the canal disappeared into a round black hole in a big stone wall. The towpath finished before it reached the tunnel, which was too narrow for a path. Nelly unhooked the rope from Clover's harness and Enoch coiled it on the boat's deck.

"Come on," Nelly said to Gertie. "We got to walk Clover over the top. We'll meet 'em at t'other end."

"Is it far to go?"

"Half a mile or so."

"But how will they get through without Clover?"

"There's a steam tug. Look, here it comes now."

With a great rattling of chains, a short boat emerged from the tunnel, belching clouds of smoke from its funnel, and a bow-legged man with a blackened face jumped off and started to hook it up to the narrowboat.

Nelly and Gertie led Clover up the steep path at the side of the cutting. As they reached the top, there was a clatter of hooves on the road and when Gertie looked back, she saw to her horror that it was the Limehouse Laundry van. The two Chinamen jumped off and ran down the path to the canal. They were in such a hurry that they did not notice Gertie, hiding her face behind Clover.

"It's them!" she hissed at Nelly. "They must have worked out that we was hidin' on your boat!"

"What're you gonna do?"

"Dunno… No, wait a minute. I got an idea…"

As they rushed down to the canal, the two men could see Wiggins and Sparrow on the boat. But they were too late – the *Betsy* disappeared into the smoke in the tunnel, and because there was no towpath, they could not follow it. Hopping with rage, they turned to climb back up to their van … only to see that it was moving off!

Sitting on the driving seat and starting up the horse was Gertie. She grabbed the whip and roused the horse into a trot, then a canter. Then, just before it broke into a gallop, she took a deep breath and jumped down. Picking herself up, she ran back to join Nelly and Clover.

Yelling at the tops of their voices, the two men chased down the road after their van. Inside it,

Shiner clung on for dear life as he was flung about, trying to work out what on earth was happening and afraid that the van might crash and turn over. The bundles of laundry were soft enough to cushion him and stop him getting hurt, but the big baskets were hard, with strong metal corners. As the van bounced over a pot-hole, Shiner was flung against one of them. He felt a bang on his head – then everything went black.

The van had gone a long way down the road before the horse eventually slowed and a police-man managed to stop it. When the men arrived, the constable said the horse must have bolted.

"Something must have spooked him," he said. "Any idea what?"

The Chinese men shrugged their shoulders and shook their heads, saying nothing about Gertie or the Boys.

"You're lucky," the policeman said, taking out his notebook. "It don't seem to have done any harm this time. Just make sure that in future you put the brake on when you leave your van unat-tended. Right? You understand?"

The men nodded, trying to look as though they were sorry.

"Best check everything's all right," the policeman said, walking slowly round the van and inspecting the wheels. "How about inside?" he asked.

They opened the back door and looked in. All they could see was a jumble of baskets and bundles. Shiner, unconscious, was lying underneath them, out of sight.

"Bit of a mess, eh?" the constable said. "You want a hand sorting it out?"

The men shook their heads. "No. We fix him back at laundry."

They bowed in thanks to the policeman then, knowing they were too late now to go back to the canal and try to catch the Boys, they climbed back onto the seat and drove away.

The smoke in the tunnel was so thick it nearly choked Wiggins and Sparrow, but Enoch didn't seem to mind it. In the olden days, he told them, when there had been no steam tugs, boatmen like his father had had to "leg" their boats through the low tunnels. They used to lie on their backs on top of the cabins, he said, and walk their feet along the roof to move the boats through.

"That was hard work, that was," Enoch said. "So I don't mind a bit of smoke, even if it does make me cough." And he proved it by lighting his pipe again and puffing contentedly as the boat went on through the darkness towards the tiny spot of light at the other end, which gradually got bigger and bigger until they emerged into the daylight again.

By the time the *Betsy* was unhooked from the tug, Nelly and Gertie had arrived with Clover, bursting to tell Wiggins and Sparrow about the Chinamen and the van. Sparrow thought it was very funny. Wiggins grinned at the idea of the men having to run after the van, but he said that even though they had shaken them off for the moment, they were still a danger. The Boys would still have to be on their guard and watch out for them, both on the journey and when they got to Limehouse.

"He's right," Enoch agreed. "Yow can't be too

careful when yow'm dealing with these foreigners. Yow'll need something to keep your strength up. How about a bit of snap?"

"Snap?" The Boys looked puzzled. "What's that?"

"Yow know – snap. Grub. Something to eat. Do yow like bacon?"

The Boys stared at him open-mouthed and nodded. Did they like bacon? The very idea made their mouths water.

"Right," Enoch said. "Nell, put the frying-pan on the stove. It's dinner time."

Shiner woke up feeling woozy and wondering where he was. At first, he couldn't understand what the bundles and baskets lying on top of him were. He struggled to push them off and sit up. His head felt sore, and when he reached up to touch it he discovered a painful lump the size of a pigeon's egg over one eye. He couldn't see anything in the dark but he could hear voices near by, jabbering away in a strange foreign language. Suddenly he remembered the Chinese men and where he was. The van was not moving now. Had they arrived? He listened carefully, trying hard to work out what was going on.

"Where have you been?" a new voice demanded in English, quiet but full of menace. "Have you brought me any new girls?"

"No can do, boss," said another voice, which sounded to Shiner like one of the two Chinese men.

"Why not?"

"Too much boys follow us. Watch us what we do."

"Boys? What sort of boys?"

"Boys from street. One called Wiggy?"

"Wiggy…? Wiggins! Those boys! Those cursed boys! Sherlock Holmes's brats. If any of them show their faces round here, deal with them. Do you hear?"

"How deal, boss?"

"Dispose of them," the man hissed. "In the river."

Shiner gulped. This was serious. They were about to open the van door, and when they did, they would see him – and he'd be done for. He would never manage to get out without being seen. He lifted the lid of one of the big baskets. It was only half full of bed sheets, leaving about enough room for a small boy. He climbed in and just managed to close the lid before the van door opened.

"Make sure the cargo is all loaded tonight," the man continued. "The ship sails on the morning tide."

"Yes, boss. We make everything ready."

"Good. And keep the rest of your men on board, where there's no risk of them giving anything away. Now get this van unloaded."

The men dragged the first big basket out, and more Chinese men appeared to help carry it away. Peering through the narrow gaps between the strands of wicker of his basket, Shiner could just make out a narrow street lined with high buildings. A tall man dressed in black was walking away towards a carriage that waited on the corner. He took off his top hat as he climbed in, revealing a shiny bald head. And as he closed the carriage door, Shiner saw a familiar monogram on it – the curly letter "M".

"Moriarty!" he whispered to himself, as the

men lifted his basket and carried it into a building, grumbling at the weight. Suddenly, Shiner was surrounded by noise – the clanging of big metal vats, the hiss of steam, unknown bangs and bumps, and the sound of loud shouting in Chinese. Trapped in his basket he couldn't see anything clearly, but he had no doubt that he was inside the Limehouse Laundry. The very home of the dreaded dragon.

In the Dragon's Den

"Here yow am, me ducks," Enoch announced in his heavy Birmingham accent. "Limehouse Basin."

Wiggins, Sparrow and Gertie looked around at the busy scene before them. The canal had opened into a big stretch of water, surrounded by tall warehouses and wharves and cranes. Its quaysides were lined with ships, boats and barges of all shapes and sizes, with dockers loading and unloading their cargoes. At the far end, a huge pair of lock gates closed off the entrance to the Thames, where they could see the masts and funnels of a big steamship passing down the river on its way to the sea.

"I'm sorry, ducks," Enoch said. "I'd like to come with yow. But we got to find our berth, and check our cargo in, and get the horse settled in the stables. You'm on your own now."

"That's all right," Wiggins replied. "Thanks for helping us. And for the snap."

"Good luck," Nelly called as they waved farewell and walked away along the quay.

"What do we do now?" Sparrow asked, staring at all the buildings and people and vessels.

"Where do we start?" Gertie joined in.

"We start," Wiggins replied, "by using our eyes."

"Yeah, but what're we lookin' for?" asked Sparrow.

"Anything unusual."

"It all looks unusual to me," said Gertie. "I never been here before."

"But the first thing we look for is the Lime-house Laundry, right?"

"Right!"

"And we better get a move on, 'cos it's gonna get dark soon."

They could see nothing in the Basin that looked anything like a laundry, and nothing that looked like a dragon's den either.

"What exac'ly did that geezer say to you about the Basin?" Wiggins asked Sparrow.

"He said if we wanted to find the girls, we have to chase the dragon, by the Basin."

"Aha!" Wiggins said in his best Sherlock Holmes manner. "*By* the Basin. Not *in* it?"

"Yeah. That's what he said, I'm sure."

"Right. Come on."

They made their way out of the entrance gates, stopping to ask the uniformed guard if he knew where the laundry was. He grinned, looking at their ragged clothes.

"Got to collect your washing, have you?" he asked.

"That's right, my man," Wiggins grinned, putting on a posh voice. "We're goin' to a ball tonight, don'tcha know?"

The guard laughed. "You wanna stick around here tonight," he said. "There's going to be a party. Some sort of Chinese festival. New Year or summat."

"Ain't got no time for parties," said Wiggins. "We got something important to do. So if you'll tell me where the laundry is…?"

"Just round the corner. Through the gates, turn left, then right. You can't miss it."

Thanking him, the Boys followed his instructions. They found themselves in a London that was very different from Baker Street. The streets were winding and narrow. The buildings were old and rickety, and their upper floors leaned towards each other as though they were looking for shared support. Many of them had signs painted on them in Chinese characters, and most of the people sitting outside or strolling along the pavements were Chinese, though there were a few who were white or black or Indian, most of whom looked like sailors.

Everywhere people were preparing for the evening's festivities, hanging brightly patterned paper lanterns from poles jutting out from the houses, and setting up food stalls. They were cooking strange-smelling dishes that reminded Sparrow of the Chinese acrobats' spicy meal in the dressing room. When an old lady picked up a morsel with chopsticks and held it out for him to taste, he put his hand to his mouth and backed away quickly, even though he was hungry.

Gertie, however, accepted a piece of meat and said it was "very tasty" and didn't burn her mouth at all. It was obviously a very different recipe from the acrobats' food, but Sparrow was still too wary to try it.

As they moved on along the street, the Boys suddenly heard a loud bang from near by. It sounded like a cannon being fired, and was followed by a lot of smaller, sharper bangs like a gun battle with revolvers. The Boys ducked down for safety, but no one else seemed scared. In fact, there was loud cheering and the sound of music from the next street: an odd sort of trumpet and the clash of cymbals and the beating of drums.

Hurrying round the corner to see what was going on, they suddenly found themselves face to face with … a dragon! Gertie and Sparrow let out a scream, and even Wiggins stepped back in fright. But they soon realized that it was not real. It was big and brightly coloured and made of paper and silk and wire. Its many legs were human – there were men inside it, dancing and weaving through the crowds and puffing smoke through the nostrils and fierce, gaping mouth.

They were tossing firecrackers on the ground to snap and bang around people's feet, making everyone jump. After their first shock, the Boys burst out laughing and hugged each other in relief.

"Cor," said Sparrow, "I thought we'd had it for a minute!"

They would have liked to follow the paper dragon and join in the fun. But they all knew they had to go on with the search for Rosie, so they turned away and carried on looking around. It didn't take long to find the Limehouse Laundry, and although they did not know it, they were soon standing on the very spot where Shiner had seen Professor Moriarty only a short time before. There was no sign now of the van, or of the two men who had chased them.

The double door to the laundry was closed, but it had windows in the upper half. Peering through, the Boys could see a number of Chinese men and women busily washing and ironing and folding bed sheets and shirts and clothes. A line of large baskets like those they had seen in the van stood against one wall, and along the back of the room there was a row of coppers: enormous metal bowls heated by big gas rings.

The Boys could not see any hint that the missing girls might be there, and they began turning away, ready to start looking somewhere else. As they did, one of the laundry workers lifted the wooden lid of one of the coppers, letting out a cloud of steam. He and another man heaved up the nearest basket and tipped its contents into the copper. Some of the boiling water splashed out onto the first man's arm. He let out a scream of pain and the other workers rushed to help him, sitting him down on the next basket in the line and fussing over his scalded arm.

"Coo, I bet that hurt," Sparrow sympathized.

Inside the basket that the man was sitting on, Shiner bit his lip and tried to stay calm. It was not easy. Through the wickerwork he had seen the men tipping the contents of the previous basket into the boiling water. What if they did the same to him? It was too horrible to think about.

At that moment, Shiner heard new voices coming into the room, loudly asking what was going on.

Wiggins, Gertie and Sparrow caught their breath as they saw two more men push their way into the laundry room through a curtained doorway at the far side.

"It's them!" Gertie exclaimed. "The fellers from the van!"

As she spoke, one of the men glanced in their direction and saw them looking through the windows. Recognizing them, he grabbed his companion's arm, pointing at the children and shouting.

"Quick!" Wiggins yelled. "Run for it!"

Ignoring the scalded man, the two men from the van charged across the laundry and out through the doors. The Boys ran for all they were worth down the street with the men in hot pursuit.

The workers in the laundry – including the man who had been scalded – rushed to the door to see what was happening. Shiner lifted the lid of his basket and peeped through the crack. All the workers were crowded in the doorway with their backs to him. He would never be able to get through the street doors without being seen, but at least he could escape from the basket – and from the steaming copper vat that awaited him. Quickly he climbed out, scurried across the room and dived behind the curtain the two men had come through. The doorway led to a dark passage and a flight of rickety stairs. He had no idea where they might lead to, but it was the only way out. With his heart beating so hard it felt as though it might burst right out of his chest, Shiner began to climb the stairs.

Out in the street, Wiggins, Sparrow and Gertie tried to push their way through the crowds enjoying the festival. But the two Chinese men were tall enough to see them over the heads of most of the people, making it hard to escape them. Glancing back, Wiggins could see that the men were gaining on them, shoving their way roughly through the crowds and even tipping over some of the food stalls.

"We ain't gonna lose 'em," Gertie panted as they came to a corner.

"Which way now?" asked Sparrow breathlessly.

"This way! Come on," said Wiggins. "Round

this corner. Stick together, now!"

They turned the corner and found it was an alleyway with no way out. And coming towards them was the paper dragon, still dancing and weaving and looking fierce.

"Oh, blimey, we're done for," Sparrow groaned. "They'll catch us now for sure."

Then he heard someone saying his name.

"Spa-ow!" a familiar voice called. "Quick! Under here!"

"What…? Who…? LI!"

The side of the dragon was lifted and the smiling face of Li, the Chinese boy from the theatre, appeared. He grabbed Sparrow's sleeve and pulled him under the cover. Other hands did the same for Wiggins and Gertie. In the dim light, Sparrow could make out the rest of the troupe of acrobats, who were working the festival dragon.

"Dance!" Li commanded.

The Boys did not need to be told twice. Taking hold of the bamboo framework inside the dragon, they copied the acrobats' steps and danced out of the alleyway, snaking past the two van men, who did not notice that the dragon had gained three extra pairs of feet.

Shiner tiptoed up the stairs, to a landing lit by a flickering, old-fashioned gas jet that left all the corners in deep black shadow. He eyed the darkness nervously – anything could be hiding there. The floorboards creaked as he stepped on them, but the firecrackers in the street outside made so much noise that it would be impossible for anyone to hear.

There were three doors on the landing. Shiner opened the nearest one very cautiously, fearful of what might be on the other side. To his relief, it led only to a small, bare storeroom. Through a window across the room he could see the lights of ships moving up and down the river, but when he tried to open it he found that it was locked shut, and in any case it was too high to jump from. The tide was out, and through the darkening gloom he could just make out an expanse of evil-looking mud below the window. If you jumped into that, he thought, it would suck you down and swallow you up like quicksand.

Shuddering at the thought, Shiner moved quickly on to the second door. Behind it was another empty room, also with a window that wouldn't open. But behind the third door was a dark and twisting passageway. Perhaps this would give him a way out. Looking and listening carefully, he crept along it and down a short flight of steps. There was yet another door at the end, and when he went through it he realized to his surprise that he must be in the next house.

The first thing Shiner noticed in the next-door house was the smell. The laundry had smelt of steam and soap and wet linen, but here it was quite different. There was a sweet, smoky aroma hanging in the air. He couldn't think what it might be, but it made him feel a bit sick, especially since he had not eaten all day. When he sniffed hard, he felt quite woozy.

Shaking his head to clear the fuzziness, Shiner started to explore. The first room he came to had three or four thin mattresses laid on the floor and a lot of Chinese clothes hanging on hooks. Against one wall was a narrow table, on which stood a picture made of beaten gold, and several small animals. One of them looked like the jade dragon from the hall of 221b Baker Street.

When he went to the window, Shiner found that this one was not locked. It faced a different direction from those he had tried in the first house, and outside, tied up to a wharf, he could see an old-fashioned ship that had masts and rigging for sails as well as a funnel for a steam engine. A crane on tall legs stood alongside it on the wharf, between the ship and the building. Its back was not far from the window, and Shiner thought he might even be able to jump out onto it, climb down and escape.

The idea of getting out and running away was very tempting. But Shiner remembered Rosie and the other flower girls, and decided that while he was in the house he had to look for them, even if it might be dangerous.

Summoning up all his courage, he crept back onto the landing and very carefully pushed open the next door along. He couldn't hear anything from inside the room, but the smoky smell was much stronger. So strong, in fact, that it almost knocked him out. He had a terrible thought –

what would a dragon's breath smell like? Could this be it?

Holding his own breath he opened the door a little wider and peeped through the gap. To his relief he saw no dragon, nor any other strange creature, though the air was heavy with yellow smoke. What he saw was a line of low wooden beds, each with a little table beside it. And on most of the beds lay men, some Chinese, some black, some white, leaning back against grubby pillows and smoking long, thin pipes with silver bowls. They all looked dreamy and sleepy. Some had their eyes closed. Others stared vacantly into space, their eyes empty as though they were not seeing anything. As Shiner watched, one of the men languidly raised an arm and muttered something and an old Chinese woman in loose black trousers and a baggy top shuffled up to him and exchanged his pipe for a new one.

Shiner was so fascinated by the scene before him that at first he did not hear someone approaching along the passageway behind. By the time he did hear, it was too late for him to back out without being seen. He thought fast and realized there was only one way he could go. The old crone had her back to him, so he nipped into the room. None of the smokers took any notice of him – they were all far, far away in their dreams.

He stood for a moment, frantically thinking what to next. As he heard the door opening again, he dropped to the floor and crawled underneath the nearest low bed. It was a tight fit, but there was just enough room. It was a good thing, he thought, that it was him and not Beaver or Wiggins, who would both have been too big. From there, he saw two pairs of feet only inches away. To Shiner, boots were as individual and recognizable as faces, and he knew at once that they belonged to the men from the van.

When the boots moved away, Shiner dared to crawl to the end of the bed, where he could see more. The two men crossed the room to a heavy door at the far end. One of them reached up and lifted a big key from a nail on the wall and unlocked the door with it. They looked back over their shoulders to check that no one was watching, then one of them went through the door and closed it behind him, leaving the other man standing guard. Shiner lay very still, watching and waiting, hardly daring to breathe.

THE TRIADS

Queenie's ankle was feeling much better after she had rested it for a while, but she was hardly thinking about that any more. It was ages since she and Beaver had seen the others running after the two Chinamen in the laundry van. Now it was dark but none of them had come back home, and Queenie was starting to get seriously worried.

She perked up hopefully as she heard footsteps on the stairs leading down to HQ. But it was only Beaver, who had been out to look for them, and he was shaking his head.

"Not a sign of 'em anywhere," he told her.

"I don't like it, Beav," Queenie said. "They should've been back by now."

"Well," he replied, trying to look on the bright side, "if they was tracking them laundry blokes they might still be after 'em. It's a long way to Limehouse, ain't it?"

"That's true. But I still don't like it."

"And if they'd found the dragon's den…"

"Ooh, don't. Anythin' might have happened. They might be scorched to a frazzle by its fiery breath…"

"But that bloke at the zoo said there weren't no such thing as dragons. And he should know."

Queenie still looked doubtful.

"I wish Mr Holmes weren't away," she said. "He'd know. He knows everythin'."

"P'raps he's back? Why don't we go and see?"

Queenie nodded. "All right. Better than sittin' 'ere mopin', I s'pose."

The festival dragon continued to wind its way through the crowds, with the men throwing firecrackers that fizzed and banged on the ground and shot off in all directions. The noise was deafening. Li gave a handful to Wiggins, telling him to throw them at the feet of anyone who got too close, to stop them looking under the cover. At last the dragon came to a halt in a quiet back alley away from the crowds. The acrobats lifted the cover from their heads and set it down on the ground.

"You did good," Li told the three Boys. "Safe now."

"Thank you," Wiggins said. "Thank you, all." He bowed to the acrobats, to show his appreciation, and Sparrow and Gertie did the same.

Sparrow looked at the man who had spoken to him backstage in the theatre and pointed at the paper-and-silk monster. "Is this the dragon you said we had to chase?" he asked.

The man looked puzzled, then shook his head and laughed. He spoke to the others, and they laughed too, as though Sparrow had said something really funny. Li listened to them, then explained to the Boys.

"He say no more dragon. Chinese say 'chasing dragon', mean smoking opium."

"Opium?" Wiggins asked.

"You know opium? Put in pipe and smoke him. Make sleepy and plenty dreamings. Called 'chasing dragon'. Chinese saying."

"Well I never," said Wiggins. "I don't know

about chasing dragons – it sounds to me like we've been on a wild-goose chase."

Now it was Li's turn to look perplexed.

"Wild goose?" he asked.

"Yeah, that's an English saying. Means wasting your time looking for something what don't exist."

"Hang on a minute," Gertie piped up. "What about Rosie? And Lily and the other girls? They exist, don't they? They ain't wild geese."

"That's right," Sparrow agreed. "And we've still gotta find 'em."

One of the men said something in Chinese.

"He say you come to right place," Li translated.

The Boys stared in astonishment.

"You mean they're here?" Wiggins asked.

"Yes. Somewhere here. But better you go home now."

"Go home?" Gertie exploded. "What's he talkin' about?"

The man said something more, then drew his finger across his throat and made a croaking sound. He looked very scared.

"Plenty bad men," Li said. "Belong triad."

"Triad?" asked Sparrow. "What's that?"

Li looked around nervously, then lowered his voice before answering.

"Triad is Chinese secret society. Plenty, plenty bad. These men belong triad called Red Fist. Big danger. Do bad things. Kill. Rob. Everything."

"Sounds like the Black Hand Gang," said Sparrow.

"Only worse," said Wiggins.

"Well, I don't care about that," Gertie cried defiantly. "I ain't scared of no Chinese tripods."

"Nor me, neither," added Sparrow. "If Rosie and Lily and the others are round here, we gotta find 'em."

"And rescue 'em," said Wiggins.

But the acrobats were clearly very scared. "Home. Go home," the first man urged, and clapped his hands over his ears, then his eyes and then his mouth.

"What's all that about?" asked Gertie.

"Hear nothing, see nothing, say nothing," said Wiggins. "He don't want nothing to do with these triads."

The man nodded vigorously. "Home," he

repeated. "Bad men kill. Go home." Then he clapped his hands and called to the others to pick up the festival dragon again. Li hung back as they climbed under the framework, desperately wanting to stay and help the Boys, but the man spoke sharply to him and pulled him into his place in the paper monster's tail. The troupe of acrobats danced away out of the alley to rejoin the street party.

"Well," said Wiggins. "Looks like we're on our own again. Up the creek wivout a paddle, as they say."

Queenie and Beaver hurried up Baker Street as fast as Queenie's injured ankle would allow. They reached number 221b just as a cab drew up in front of the house, bringing Sherlock Holmes and Dr Watson home from solving the great detective's latest case.

"Mr Holmes! Doctor!" Queenie shouted at the top of her voice. "We gotta see you! It's urgent!"

The two men turned and stared at them in surprise.

"Why, it's Queenie. And Beaver," Mr Holmes

said. "And I see you've been in the wars."

"Tripped over," Queenie replied. "It's nothin', really."

"Come inside and I'll take a look at it," said Dr Watson.

"That ain't why we've come," Queenie said. "We gotta talk to Mr Holmes. It's a matter of life and death."

"That's right," Beaver joined in. "A matter of life and death."

"It must be, to bring you out at this time of night," said Dr Watson. "Can't it wait till morning?"

"No, sir. It can't. And nobody else will listen to us."

"Very well," said Mr Holmes. "In that case, I shall."

A sleepy-looking Billy, wearing a dressing gown over his nightshirt, had opened the door and was holding it for them while the cabbie lifted down two leather suitcases and Dr Watson paid him his fare. Mr Holmes nodded to Billy and paused as he passed him.

"You may bring up the bags, Billy," he said.

"And then tell me why you are so concerned about the absent jade carving. And how it is connected to the matter my young friends wish to speak of."

"How did you…?" Billy gasped.

"I have eyes, Billy, and I use them. I observed your troubled glance at the space on the hall table where Mrs Hudson's jade dragon usually stands. And I saw Queenie look at it too. Now why is she so interested, I wonder?"

"'Cos it was a dragon," Queenie blurted out.

"Hmmm. I must confess, the significance of that remark escapes me. But no doubt you will enlighten me in due course. Come along." And with that, Mr Holmes bounded ahead, leaving Dr Watson to help Queenie hobble up the stairs and settle her on the sofa in the living room.

While Billy brought up the cases and Dr Watson fetched his medical bag and examined Queenie's ankle, Beaver and Queenie told Mr Holmes everything that had happened. He listened with great interest as they described the disappearance of Rosie and the other flower girls, right up to the moment when Queenie fell down as they were following the laundry van.

"Don't forget the perfessor," Beaver reminded Queenie.

"The perfessor – er, professor?" Mr Holmes asked. "Do you by any chance mean Professor Moriarty?"

"Yes, sir. The very same. When we come out of Bow Street nick, we see his carriage goin' round the corner. Like he'd been watching us."

"Aha!" Mr Holmes exclaimed. "I might have guessed at the involvement of that scoundrel. No doubt that explains the theft of the jade from this house."

"How's that, sir?" asked Billy.

"It is clearly a taunt, directed at me. Something in the nature of a challenge."

"You mean he came here, sir? Into this house?"

"I do not suppose he came in person. It would be more likely that he sent some henchman. Ah," his eyebrows shot up his forehead. "I have it. Which laundry does Mrs Hudson employ?"

"We have a new one, sir. A Chinese laundry from Limehouse."

"There is your answer. There is no need for

Mrs Hudson to blame you, Billy. This is undoubtedly a small part of a dastardly plot. It would appear that Professor Moriarty has availed himself of the services of a band of Oriental criminals. What is referred to in China as a triad. This is indeed a most serious business. Now, Queenie, Beaver. You must think very hard and try to remember everything. Every detail may be important in solving this crime."

"We told you everything, sir," said Queenie.

"Yes, I'm sure you have." He pondered for a moment, thinking hard, then his face lightened. "Tell me again," he said, "exactly what the Chinese acrobat said to Sparrow at the theatre."

"He said if we wanted to find our friends we had to go lookin' for the dragon, what was by the bowl."

"There is a silver bowl on the hall table, where the jade dragon stood," suggested Dr Watson. "Could that be what he was referring to, I wonder?"

Mr Holmes did not answer but paced the room, thinking hard. Then he turned, with one finger raised.

"Looking for the dragon?" he asked. "Were those his exact words?"

"We had to go chasing it, I think that's what Sparrow said."

"Ha! That puts a very different complexion on the matter."

"Beg pardon, sir?"

"That changes everything. I have it, I have it!" he cried triumphantly. "Watson, if you would be so good as to hand me the book of tide tables from the shelf near your elbow…?"

Mr Holmes opened the book that the doctor passed to him and swiftly ran a finger down the columns of figures on its pages.

"These tables," he explained, "give the exact times of the tides which raise and lower the level of the River Thames by several feet each day. Hmm… Billy, kindly run and find us a cab, as quickly as you can. We have not a moment to lose."

Shiner felt as though he had been hiding under the low bed for hours and he was finding it hard to stay awake. His head ached from the bump he had received, and the smoke from the opium pipes was making him increasingly sleepy. He was just beginning to nod off when the door opened at last and he saw the feet of the second man going into the room to join his accomplice. Stretching forward as far as he dared, Shiner watched the two men come out carrying something heavy between them, wrapped in a blanket. They locked the door behind them and hung the key on its nail high up on the wall. None of the smokers dozing on the beds paid any attention as the two men carried their burden out of the room.

Shiner waited for a little while, to make quite sure they had gone, then silently eased himself out and crawled to the locked door. The old crone was sitting at a table with her back to him, busy slicing pieces off a block of something brown with a wicked-looking cleaver. He stood up slowly and reached for the key. It was too high for him. He tried a little jump but still couldn't reach it, and his feet made a noise when he landed back on the floor. Holding his breath, he stood very still. Had the old woman heard?

Would she look round and see him?

When she did not move, Shiner reached across the nearest empty bed, picked up the little table and placed it below the key. He wondered if it would be strong enough to support his weight – it looked a bit flimsy – but decided he had to try. To his relief, it didn't collapse when he climbed onto it. He was even more relieved to find that he could reach the key. He lifted it off its nail, stepped down and put it into the keyhole.

The key turned easily in the lock, and when Shiner pushed the door, it opened without a sound. Slipping inside, he closed it behind him. The room he found himself in was darker than the one he had just left, and the one window was boarded up with thick planks. It took a few moments for his eyes to get used to the gloom, but gradually he was able to make out a row of bunk beds around the walls. At first he thought they were all empty, but then he saw there was someone or something lying on one of the bottom bunks. He tiptoed across to it. It was a girl. She was lying very still, with her back to him. He reached out and shook her shoulder, very carefully. She did not move. Was she asleep – or something worse? He bent over her to see her face. It was Rosie.

THE MORNING TIDE

Wiggins, Sparrow and Gertie watched the festival dragon snake its way back down the alley, leaving them alone in the darkness. It was late, and the sounds of the celebrations were dying down as the revellers made their way home.

"Where do we start, then?" Sparrow asked.

"Back at the laundry," Wiggins said. "But keep your eyes peeled for them triad geezers. From what your friend said, they'd slit our throats and dump us in the river if we give 'em half a chance."

"Huh! I'd like to see 'em try," said Gertie bravely.

"I wouldn't," said Sparrow.

"Nor me," Wiggins agreed. "So watch your backs. Come on."

They crept out of the alley and looked very carefully to the left and right. Then, trying to remember the route they'd taken when they were inside the dragon, they set off in the direction of the laundry, keeping close to the walls of the houses and walking in single file. As there were so few people about now, the Boys had no chance of hiding themselves among the crowds, so they stayed in the shadows.

After a couple of wrong turns they found themselves standing outside the laundry. All the lights had been turned off apart from one small gas jet at the back, which cast a dim glimmer, just enough to show that the workers had left for the day. The doors were firmly locked and bolted. If the girls were somewhere inside, there was no way the Boys could get in to find them.

"Now what do we do?" Gertie wondered.

"P'raps there's a way in round the back," suggested Sparrow.

"Good thinking, lad," said Wiggins. "Trouble is, I reckon these houses back straight on to the river."

"Sure, and that's all right," grinned Gertie. "I can swim."

"Yeah, but I can't," Sparrow groaned.

"Nor me," said Wiggins. "Never mind. Let's see what we can find."

Rosie was breathing, but she was so deeply asleep that she must have been drugged. Shiner shook her and patted her face and whispered in her ear, but he couldn't wake her up. He tried to lift her but she was too heavy for him, and even if he could have carried her he would not have been able to get her out of the house without being seen. It was a terrible quandary. He hated the thought of leaving her – and if he did, who could tell what might happen to her? But if he stayed until the men came back, they would catch him too, and then he would be no use at all. He decided that the only thing he could do was to try and get away himself and find help from someone, somewhere.

Shiner slipped back out of the room, locking the door behind him so that if the men came back they would not see that he had been there.

He was just climbing onto the little table to put the key back on its hook when the old woman spotted him.

"Hey!" she shouted. "Who you? What you do?"

She stood up, brandishing her razor-sharp cleaver menacingly. As she started towards him, Shiner raced for the door, bumping into one of the beds on the way and tipping it over. The smoker fell onto the floor in the path of the old woman, slowing her down and giving Shiner a useful start.

On the landing, Shiner remembered the unlocked window in the other room. He rushed in, heaved it open and climbed onto the sill. The crane seemed to be much further away than it had been before, and the wharf looked a very long way down. But he had no time to worry about falling. If he didn't get out, he would be captured. Taking a deep breath, he jumped.

Wiggins, Sparrow and Gertie walked along the street until they discovered a gap in the buildings. It was pitch-black in the long narrow space, but at the far end they could see flickers of light reflecting from water as dawn approached, and could just make out a flight of worn stone steps leading down towards a wharf. Feeling their way with care and walking one behind the other, they advanced nervously down the ancient stairway. Suddenly, ahead of them, they heard the sound of bolts being drawn back and a patch of light spilled onto the steps as a door opened in the side wall on the left. A dark shadow loomed across it as a man stepped out. He was carrying something heavy wrapped in what looked like a blanket.

The Boys pressed themselves against the wall and froze, not daring to breathe as they recognized one of the men from the laundry van standing only a few feet away from them. A moment later the other man came out and closed the door behind him, then both men clambered down the steps, sharing the burden of whatever was in the blanket. When they reached the bottom and turned out of sight, Wiggins crept down and peeped round the corner. He beckoned to the others to join him.

"It's the Basin," he whispered. "The Lime-house Basin. Look."

Everything was quiet in the Basin. Most of the ships and boats were in darkness with their crews still sleeping. The Boys could see the two Chinese men humping their load across the wharf under the legs of a big crane towards a ship, where a seaman holding a lantern waited for them at the top of the gangway.

"What d'you think they're carryin'?" Sparrow asked. "D'you think it could be…?"

The three Boys looked at each other, not daring to say what they thought and feared. But Sparrow's question was soon answered. As the men climbed up the gangway, something flopped out of the blanket and dangled below it. It was an arm. A girl's arm, wearing a flowery sleeve, looking very pale and white in the lantern's light. One of the men leant over and tucked it back inside the blanket, then they reached the deck and disappeared into the ship.

The Boys were silent for a moment.

"I gotta get on board that ship," Wiggins muttered. "Find out what's going on."

"We'll come with you," said Sparrow.

"No. You two wait and keep an eye on things

from here. If I don't come back, raise the alarm."

He was just about to dart across the wharf when another man came out of the passageway and scurried across to the ship and up the gangway. As he reached the top, the seaman with the lantern reappeared and the new man spoke urgently to him in Chinese, waving his arms and pointing back to the buildings. Then he hurried inside the ship, leaving the man with the lantern standing guard by the rail.

"Now what?" asked Gertie.

"There's gotta be another way of getting aboard," said Wiggins. "I'm gonna take a look."

The day was dawning quickly now, with streaks of silver and gold brightening the sky. Wiggins knew he would have to move fast if he was to make use of the last of the darkness and not be seen. Dodging between packing cases and piles of sacks waiting to be loaded, he reached the crane near the ship's bow and ducked behind its nearest leg while he eyed the mooring rope that was looped around a bollard on the wharf. He was sizing up the rope, wondering if he could climb up it and whether he would be able to get on board that way, when he heard a strange sound.

"*Pssst!*" it went. "*Pssst!*" And then an urgent whisper: "Wiggins!"

He stopped. Who could it be? How did whoever it was know his name?

"*Psssst!*" it came again. "Up here!"

He looked up, and saw a small figure perched on the metal framework of the crane, silhouetted against the lightening sky.

"It's me," the figure hissed. "Shiner."

"Shiner! What you doing up there?"

"Watchin'. Come on up – there's a ladder running up the crane leg."

Wiggins didn't have a good head for heights, but this was no time to give in to such weaknesses. He found the ladder leading up to the crane driver's cab and climbed it, step by step, holding on very tight and taking care not to make a noise with his boots on the thin iron rungs. Shiner was waiting for him at the top, sitting on the metal frame, hidden from the ship by the cab.

"How d'you get here?" Wiggins asked him.

"I come through that window," Shiner whispered, jerking his thumb at the house behind the crane.

Wiggins looked puzzled. "No," he said, "I mean here. Limehouse. How did you…? Oh, never mind. You can tell me later."

"Listen – they got Rosie in there. I seen her."

"Why didn't you get her out?"

"Couldn't shift her. They must have give her some knock-out drops or somethin'. Then this old biddy went for me wiv a chopper, and I had to run for it."

"So Rosie's still in there?"

"I dunno for sure. They might have fetched her."

"What about the other girls?"

"I think they're on that ship."

"Did you see them?"

"No. But I seen Moriarty. He told them laundry men to get the cargo on board quick, 'cos the ship's sailin' on the morning tide."

"The cargo? That must be the girls."

"Yeah. And it's mornin' already. What we gonna do?"

"We got no time to lose. We gotta get on board and find 'em."

"Yeah, but how we gonna do that?"

Wiggins pointed to the arm of the crane. It had been swung out over the ship, ready to load the last few bits of cargo, and the hook was dangling only a few feet above the deck.

"If I work my way along to the end," he said, "I reckon I can climb down the rope."

Shiner grinned. "That's clever. Let's go."

"What d'you mean? You're not coming."

"Well, I ain't stoppin' here. Go on. It'll be light soon."

Wiggins shrugged, nodded, then started crawling along the arm, trying to forget how high up he was. By the time he reached the end, he was trembling with nerves. But he gritted his teeth, swung himself onto the cable and shinned down it to the hook. Then he dropped lightly on to the deck and crouched behind a hatch cover. Shiner followed. As soon as they had got their breath back they crept across to the far side of the ship, away from the watchman and the quayside, and tiptoed along until they found a door.

Wiggins was just about to try the door when it flew open, almost in his face. He and Shiner were nearly squashed behind it – but at least it hid them. From inside came the sound of men's voices, speaking in a foreign language. The boys stood very still as a dark-skinned man wearing a vest and grubby white trousers came out holding a bucket full of slops, which he slung over the rail and into the water of the Basin. Then he went back inside and pulled the door shut behind him.

The two Boys breathed again and moved on. A little further along they found another door, which they opened very cautiously. To their relief there were no men inside it, only a staircase, leading down into the body of the ship.

"They'll have 'em down there, I reckon," whispered Wiggins. "Come on."

As they started down the stairs, there was a loud hissing of steam and clanking noises and the dinging of a bell from far beneath them. They looked at each other in alarm, then hurried on. The stairs ended in a long corridor, with many doors on either side. The Boys began opening them and looking inside. Most of them seemed to be cabins. In the first one they found two men in bunk beds. Fortunately they were asleep and did not hear or see them. Pulling the door shut, they carried on, Wiggins taking one side of the corridor and Shiner the other, to make it quicker.

When they reached the end of the corridor they had still found no sign of the girls, but they came to another flight of stairs, this time so steep it was more like a ladder. They scrambled down it and found themselves facing an iron door. Instead of a lock or handle, it had a wheel in the middle. Wiggins turned it, swung the door open and saw a big dark space. As his eyes got used to the dim light he could make out a line of pale white faces staring out at him.

At that moment, from both above and below, there was more hissing and clanking, and the sound of men's voices shouting orders. Then they felt the whole ship judder and sway.

"Oh, lawks!" Wiggins exclaimed. "It's moving! The ship's moving!"

Sparrow and Gertie, crouching in the opening between the buildings, looked on in horror as the ship came to life before their eyes. Steam spurted, smoke belched out of the tall black funnel and bells rang. Seamen hurried down onto the wharf, unhitched the mooring ropes from the bollards then ran back on board. As they pulled up the gangway, the ship was already moving away from the quay, churning the water at its stern as the gap grew wider and wider.

Sparrow and Gertie could not stay hidden while their friends were carried away. They rushed out of the passage, waving their arms and shouting to the ship to stop. It was getting quite light now, but no one saw or heard them – or if they did they took no notice. Within a very short time, the ship was in the middle of the Basin and heading for the river.

"Now what we gonna do?" wailed Gertie.

"I know!" yelled Sparrow. "Enoch!"

They raced off along the quayside and soon spotted the *Betsy* lying quietly at its mooring. The painted doors to the cabin were closed, but Sparrow leapt down into the cockpit and hammered on them as hard as he could. There was a shout from inside, and Enoch's head appeared in the doorway, his eyes blinking sleepily.

"What the…?" he mumbled. "What the Dickens is going on?"

"Enoch, Enoch, you've gotta help us," Gertie gabbled. "That ship. We gotta stop it!"

"They're takin' Wiggins and the girls!" Sparrow cried.

"Whoa! Whoa! Hold your horses," Enoch said. "Now, take a breath and tell me what's up."

"The girls we told you about … they're on that ship…" Gertie panted, pointing frantically at the ship.

"And Wiggins went after 'em and now he's on it as well and it's sailing, look!" Sparrow cried.

Enoch was wide awake now. He disappeared briefly into the cabin, then emerged again pulling on his trousers and boots.

"It's all right," he said. "They'm still in the Basin and they can't get out till the lock gates…" He stopped, and stared across the water. "Oh no. It's high tide, so the gates are open. We gotta get 'em shut or they can sail right out. Come on!"

Still tucking his shirt into his trousers, he set off along the quay. Behind him, Nell came tumbling out of the cabin, wrapping a shawl over her nightdress. The four of them galloped along the quayside as fast as they could go, shouting at the tops of their voices to the lock keeper. But it was no use. The ship was picking up speed, and before they could get to the open gates, it was passing through. They could only stand by the side, gasping for breath, and watch helplessly as it turned into the river and headed towards the sea.

MEN OVERBOARD

On the ship, Wiggins was trying to calm down the kidnapped girls as they clustered round him. One or two were still lying on their bunks, drowsy from the drugs, but the rest of them were very excited at seeing the two Boys. One of the girls even flung her arms around Wiggins and kissed him, to his great embarrassment. Shiner stepped back quickly in case any of them tried to do the same to him, but fortunately none of them did.

"Girls! Girls!" Wiggins said in a hoarse whisper. "Take it easy. Now we've found you, we gotta find a way of getting you out of here."

"How are you gonna do that?" asked the girl who was still clinging to him. "Is this all there is of you?"

"There's more of us on the side. We're the Baker Street Boys."

"What, Rosie's lot?"

"That's us."

"Where is Rosie? Have you rescued her already?"

"Ain't she here? I thought we just seen 'em carrying her on board."

"That was Lily. Look, she's just comin' round now."

Behind her, Wiggins could see Lily waking up and peering around her in the gloom. "Rosie?" she mumbled. "Where's Rosie?"

"Shhh ... don't fret about Rosie," said Wiggins, trying to calm her, though he felt anything but calm himself. "If she ain't here, we know where to find her. Right, Shiner?"

"That's right," Shiner agreed. "I seen her."

"Now," Wiggins told the girls, "I want you to stop here and keep quiet while Shiner and me go up top to see what's what. OK?"

The girls were not happy at being left in their prison, even with the door open, but they nodded reluctantly. Wiggins and Shiner set off back along the corridors and up the stairways until they reached the deck.

"Blimey," Wiggins cried, grabbing the rail and looking out. "We ain't in the Basin no more – we're on the river!"

They were so shocked that they did not see one of the big Chinamen from the laundry coming round the corner. But he saw them, and let out an angry roar.

"Run for it!" Wiggins told Shiner. But as they turned to run away along the deck, they found themselves facing the second big Chinaman, who came round the other corner ahead of them. There were only two ways for them to go: over the side and into the river, where they would drown, or up the rigging, which was very high.

Wiggins glanced up at the masts, which looked so tall they seemed to disappear into the morning river mist, and swallowed hard. But Shiner was already climbing and Wiggins caught hold of a rope and did the same. It was like climbing a rope ladder that swayed and swung alarmingly as they scrambled upwards, higher and higher, and both Boys were terrified of losing their footing and falling. Below them on the deck the two men grinned up at them, their dark eyes glittering with evil glee as they prepared to follow.

Wiggins thought desperately. If the men caught them they would knock them down onto the hard deck, or hurl them overboard into the swirling waters of the Thames. They had no weapons to defend themselves with. What could they do? Then he remembered the firecrackers that Li and the acrobats had given him to use during the dragon dance. He still had a string of them in his jacket pocket. Hooking an arm through the ropes, he pulled it out, yanked at the self-lighting fuse, then flung it onto their pursuers below. The men yelled, then leapt off the rigging as the crackers began to explode around them with a series of loud bangs.

"What on earth...? Sounds like gunfire!" exclaimed Doctor Watson.

"It appears to be coming from that ship that has just left the Basin," said Mr Holmes. "What do you make of it, Inspector?"

Inspector Hunter of the Thames River Police

lifted his binoculars and trained them on the ship.

"Can't see any guns," he said. "But there certainly appears to be something amiss. There are people in the rigging. Sergeant, steer towards that vessel."

Beaver and Queenie clung on hard as the police steam launch heeled over, powering towards the ship at top speed. They had enjoyed the ride down the river from Westminster, watching the dawn sky paint first the water and then the great dome of St Paul's Cathedral and the stone walls of the Tower of London with light. And they had been thrilled to pass under the gleaming new Tower Bridge and into the Pool of London, packed with sleeping ships and flat barges and lighters, all waiting to start another day in the life of the busiest docks in the world.

Mr Holmes had asked Scotland Yard to send policemen to Limehouse by road. But he had guessed that the villains would try to escape by water, and so he had taken more constables on board the launch to approach the Basin from the river. They would have sailed straight into the

Basin if they had not been alerted by Wiggins's firecrackers.

"Unless I am mistaken," Mr Holmes said, "that person in the rigging looks very much like my young friend Wiggins. Inspector, if I may borrow your binoculars, please…"

The inspector handed them over and Mr Holmes quickly focused them on the ship.

"Just as I thought," he said. "Wiggins, without a doubt."

"And the other one's Shiner!" said Queenie.

"You can tell without the glasses?"

"I could tell my little brother anywhere. Hold on a minute… Look at that lot. Hey – it's the flower girls!"

There was a sudden flurry of movement on the ship as the girls, tired of waiting and scared by the bangs, burst out of the door and onto the deck. When they saw the two big Chinamen, they let out wild shrieks and charged at them, driving them back against the rail. Faced with a dozen angry girls, all eager for revenge, the two men considered possible ways to escape, then flung themselves over the side and into the water.

"Stand by to rescue men overboard," the inspector ordered calmly. "And to arrest them." Then he picked up a megaphone and pointed it at the ship. "This is the police," he boomed. "Heave to at once and prepare to be boarded!"

Gertie and Sparrow were waiting by the lock gates with Enoch and Nell when the police launch brought the other four Boys back to shore, with Mr Holmes and Dr Watson. The flower girls were still on the ship, which was making its way back to the Basin more slowly.

"Is this the lot of yow?" Enoch asked as they greeted each other. "All safe and sound now?"

"No," cried Gertie. "Where's Rosie?"

"Is she still on the ship?" asked Sparrow. "Why haven't you brought her with you?"

Gertie let out an anguished howl. "What's happened to Rosie? Is she all right?"

"We don't know yet," Queenie said.

"But I know where to find her," said Shiner. "Leastways, I hope she's still there."

He pointed up at the boarded-up window next to the one he had escaped through.

"Come along, then," said Mr Holmes. "No time to lose if she's still in their clutches. Watson – you brought your service revolver, I trust?"

Dr Watson nodded and patted his coat pocket.

"Excellent. Keep it to hand – we may have need of it if these brutes turn nasty."

"How do we get up there?" Queenie asked.

"We know that," Sparrow said. "This way."

He and Gertie led the way up the steps in the narrow passageway and into the street.

"Look!" Beaver exclaimed. "The Limehouse Laundry."

"Yeah, but she weren't in there," Shiner said. "She was in this house, next door."

Mr Holmes nodded. "Exactly as I thought," he said. "I know this place – it is one of the most notorious opium dens in London, the favourite haunt of those poor wretches who spend their time chasing the dragon."

"You know about that?" Wiggins asked.

"Indeed I do. As soon as I heard that phrase I knew where to look. But you had to work it out for yourselves. I congratulate you. Shall we go in?"

He led the way up a flight of rickety stairs and

pushed open the door to the smoking room. The old crone looked up and took hold of her cleaver, but she put it down again when Dr Watson drew the revolver from his pocket. Mr Holmes glared sternly at her and raised a warning finger. While the other Boys stared in astonishment at the opium addicts dreaming on their beds, Shiner hurried across to the room where he had seen Rosie. Mr Holmes followed, lifted the key from its nail and handed it to him.

Shiner's hand trembled with nerves as he unlocked the door and looked inside, fearful of what he might find. But to his delight he found Rosie, sitting up on the narrow bed and looking sleepy but unharmed.

"You took your time getting here," she said. "What kept you?"

The police launch sounded three loud whoops on its hooter as it steamed out of the Limehouse Basin. Enoch and Nell watched from the side of the lock as they passed through, and Li and the acrobats ran up just in time to join them in waving goodbye to the Boys.

"Case closed," said Wiggins contentedly. "Time to go home, back to HQ."

"You have done well," Mr Holmes praised him. "You have foiled Moriarty's villainous schemes once again. I am truly proud of you."

Inspector Lestrade's men had arrived soon after Shiner had released Rosie, and had begun arresting the big Chinamen's accomplices in the laundry and the opium den. The inspector had found an omnibus to carry the flower girls back to their homes, after Dr Watson had examined them and declared that they had come to no harm.

"They appear to have been put to sleep by the administration of laudanum," he said. "Which, as you may know, is a tincture of opium. I am happy to say that it will cause them no lasting injury."

As a special reward for their efforts, the Boys were returning to the West End on the launch, and Beaver and Queenie were pleased to be able to point out to the others all the famous places they had seen earlier, on their journey down the river to Limehouse. As they passed under Tower Bridge they were all very excited to see the roadway over their heads being raised to allow a big ship to sail through. And they were chilled when Dr Watson pointed out Traitor's Gate in the Tower of London and told them how prisoners were taken through it to be beheaded.

"That's what they oughta do to Perfesser Moriarty," said Shiner.

"If the police ever manage to catch him," said Mr Holmes. "Which I very much doubt. He is far too slippery to leave any incriminating evidence behind him."

"But I seen him!" Shiner cried. "I seen him with them Chinamen."

"But what did you see? He could have been delivering his dirty linen to the laundry."

"And we saw him in Covent Garden, by Bow Street nick," added Beaver.

"Driving along a public street in his carriage. Where is the crime in that?"

"You're right," said Wiggins. "He always gets somebody else to do his dirty work, don't he?"

"He does indeed, my dear Wiggins. In the present case, he enlisted the help of the Chinese gangsters known as the triads. Normally these criminals prey only upon their innocent fellow countrymen, and London's Chinatown will be a better place without them. But Moriarty clearly persuaded them to break with tradition and attack a helpless section of the English population."

"The flower girls!" said Sparrow.

"Precisely. One of whom – Rosie here – happens to be a member of my Baker Street Boys. Kidnapping her, from under my very nose as it were, would be one in the eye for Mr Sherlock Holmes, would it not?"

"And that's why they took Mrs Hudson's jade dragon!" said Wiggins.

"Exactly. As an affront, a challenge – which you took up on my behalf and, I am happy to say, won handsomely."

"But what exac'ly was they up to?"

"I have no doubt they intended to transport the girls to the mysterious Orient, or to North Africa, say, where they would have sold them as slaves. A pretty white girl would bring a good price for the palace of some sultan or emperor."

"Well I never," said Queenie, shocked.

"Cor," said Rosie, gulping as she imagined

herself as a slave, locked away behind high walls for ever. "I wouldn't like that very much."

"No," said Mr Holmes, "I'm quite sure you wouldn't."

"But how come they didn't take me on the ship with the others?"

"Clearly their plan was interrupted by something – or someone."

"You mean us?" Wiggins asked.

"Precisely. They feared you were about to expose them. So they decided to cut their operation short and make a run for it."

"And leave Rosie behind?"

"They had no time to go back for her without the risk of being seen. I have no doubt that the remaining members of the gang would have ensured her silence. Permanently."

"Oh, the scoundrels! The wicked fiends!" said Dr Watson.

"Crikey," said Rosie. "Sounds like I've had a lucky escape either way."

"Indeed you have," said Mr Holmes. "And we should celebrate your escape, along with another triumph for the Baker Street Boys. What do you all say to a slap-up feast tonight? I know a very good Chinese restaurant."

Sparrow replied for everyone. "Ta very much," he said, "but I'd rather have a nice plate of boiled beef and carrots…"

Late that night, with Rosie safely tucked up in her own bed and the others fast asleep with stomachs full of beef steaks and pork chops and mutton cutlets followed by treacle puddings and jam roly-poly and lashings of ice cream, Beaver sat down at the big table in HQ and opened his exercise book at a clean page. Queenie limped across to him and peeped over his shoulder.

"What you gonna call this one?" she asked. "'The Case of the Dragon's Den'?"

"I dunno. What about 'The Case of the Lime-house Laundry'?"

"Yes, that's nice. Goodnight, then." And with that she made her way to her bed.

Beaver licked the end of his pencil and started to write.

COVENT GARDEN AND LIMEHOUSE

COVENT GARDEN was London's main centre for fruit, vegetables and flowers for hundreds of years until 1974, when the market was moved to Nine Elms on the other side of the River Thames. The old market halls still stand and are now filled with restaurants, shops and museums, while the Piazza sees regular shows by street performers, including jugglers and acrobats. The beautiful Floral Hall, where Rosie bought her flowers in this story, is now part of the Royal Opera House, opposite the famous Bow Street police station. The area is now one of the city's most popular tourist centres and attracts visitors from all over the world.

LIMEHOUSE was London's first Chinatown, home to Chinese sailors who came ashore from ships in the nearby docks. The Chinese population moved away long ago, to Soho in the West End. But Limehouse Basin is still there. It is now a marina for yachts and pleasure boats, including many narrowboats. Regent's Canal still ends in the Basin. It runs across London from Paddington, past the zoo and Camden Lock and through the long tunnel under Islington. The boats that use it all have engines and no longer need horses to pull them along, or tugs to tow them through the tunnels. And the narrowboats no longer carry cargo. Most of them have been converted into houseboats, with comfortable cabins stretching the whole length of the boat instead of the tiny space that people like Enoch and Nell had to live in.